P9-CKR-629

THE

INTO THE WIND

WILLIAM LOIZEAUX

with illustrations by Laura Jacobsen

Egremont, Massachusetts

One Elm Books is an imprint of Red Chair Press LLC
www.oneelmbooks.com
www.redchairpress.com

Discussion Guide available online.

Publisher's Cataloging-In-Publication Data

Names: Loizeaux, William, author. | Jacobsen, Laura, illustrator.

Title: Into the wind / William Loizeaux ; with illustrations by Laura Jacobsen.

Description: Egremont, Massachusetts : One Elm Books, [an imprint of Red Chair Press LLC], [2021] | Includes a glossary of key sailing terms. | Interest age level: 009-012. | Summary: "Into the Wind is a middle-grade novel about the unlikely friendship between a boy and an elderly woman"--Provided by publisher.

Identifiers: ISBN 9781947159426 (library hardcover) | ISBN 9781947159389 (PDF) | ISBN 9781947159457 (ePub)

Subjects: LCSH: Children and older people--Juvenile fiction. | Friendship--Juvenile fiction. | Sailing--Juvenile fiction. | CYAC: Children and adults--Fiction. | Friendship--Fiction. | Sailing--Fiction.

Classification: LCC PZ7.L8295 In 2021 (print) | LCC PZ7.L8295 (ebook) | DDC [Fic]--dc23

LC record available at https://lccn.loc.gov/2019957520

This book is a work of fiction. Any references to historical events, real people or real places are used fictitiously. Other names, characters, places, and events are products of the author's imagination, and any resemblance to actual events, places, or persons, living or dead is entirely coincidental.

Main body text set in Adobe Caslon Pro 13/18.5

Text copyright by William Loizeaux
Copyright © 2021 Red Chair Press LLC

RED CHAIR PRESS, ONE ELM Books logo, and green leaf colophon are registered trademarks of Red Chair Press LLC.

All rights reserved. No part of this book may be reproduced, stored in an information or retrieval system, or transmitted in any form by any means, electronic, mechanical including photocopying, recording, or otherwise without the prior written permission from the Publisher. For permissions, contact info@redchairpress.com

Printed in Canada

0820 1P S21FN

For Beth, Emma, Chester, Meg, and Chris

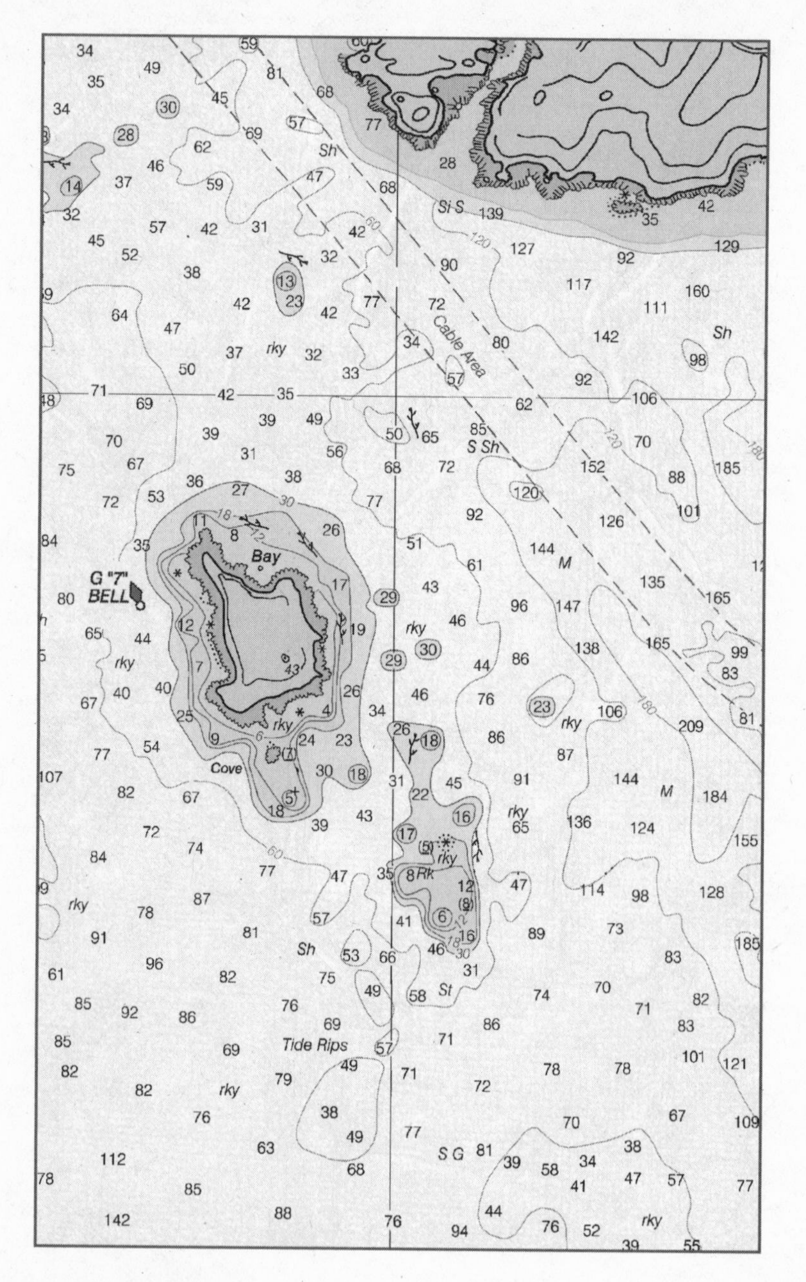

Cable Area
Bay
Cove
G "7"
BELL
Tide Rips
Si S
S Sh
Sh
rky
Rk
St
S G
M

CHAPTER 1

Hazel

"Hey, kid!" a gravelly voice called from behind me.

Startled, I turned from bailing the afternoon's rain out of my sailboat and saw this creepy old lady about fifteen feet away on the dock, not far from where I'd left my bike. She was sitting in a wheelchair and looking straight at me.

"Kid!" she called again, rolling right up to my boat and touching it with the toes of her rubber-soled shoes. "This boat, is it yours?"

I recognized her, though I didn't know her name. She owned the Art Barn, a tiny garage on Main Street, where she sold her paintings of the beach and the bay to the vacationers who take the ferry to our island from the mainland. "Yes," I said. And I almost said *Would you get your feet off my boat?*

"Will you take me out in it?" she asked. Up close like that, she looked scary, her pink scalp showing beneath her wiry white hair, her hands knobby, her chin whiskery, her face wrinkly and gray as driftwood. She wore a baggy blue sweat suit. "Will you take me sailing?"

Mom and Dad have always told my sister Lizzy and me to be "nice" to old people, and Lizzy, being so smart and perfect *at everything*, would have found some nice way to get out of this situation. But I just looked down at my soaked sneakers and hoped this old lady would roll herself back down the dock and let me get on with my work.

She didn't move. "Kid, will you take me?"

I tried to put her off: "Maybe. Sometime."

"Why not now?"

Was she kidding? My boat is an old catboat, beat-up but beautiful. It isn't much bigger than a rowboat, so even if I wanted to take her sailing, how in the world would I get her and her wheelchair aboard? Couldn't she see that the boat was still full of water? "Look," I said, "my sail's all rolled up. When I'm done bailing, I have to go."

She cocked her head like a seagull. "Where?"

"I have things to do."

"Oh?" One of her wispy eyebrows shot up. "Like what?"

"Things... Like homework. Math."

At this, she cracked up laughing, a kind of cackling sound, throwing back her white head, so I saw that some of her back teeth were missing. "Homework? Ha! On a beautiful afternoon like this? In the *summer*?"

Unfortunately, it was true. I *did* have homework—usually. I'd failed math a few weeks before, after it got hard to concentrate on anything. So now I had to go to summer school, and I had to pass the course to start sixth grade with the rest of my class in September. It was also true that on that particular day, the day after the Fourth of July, I didn't actually have any homework.

Now the lady was shaking her head slowly in disbelief, like I didn't even know how to tell a good lie.

"Look, I don't know why you're asking me all these questions," I said. "I hardly know you."

"I've seen you around," she replied, not laughing anymore. "And every now and then your mom comes into my shop, just to look around." She paused, thinking. The wrinkles on her forehead tightened. "But I haven't seen her for a while."

What did *she* know about my mom? And how was

it any of *her* business? I looked across the dark blue of the bay and the darker blue of the sound toward the mainland, a thin green line, like a thread, on the horizon. Trying to focus again on bailing, I started scooping and pouring, faster and faster, scooping and pouring, scooping and pouring… In my boat there are always things like this that I can do, things I can fix, things I can take care of—unlike some of the other things that I couldn't do anything about.

Like she had nothing better to do, the old lady just sat there and watched me bail. Along with the scooping and pouring, there was the rocking of the low waves, the *squinch* of the rubber fenders against the dock, the screams of the gulls, the sticky, salty smell of the breeze, and the late-afternoon sun baking my back. Ten minutes later, she still hadn't moved, and it was getting more and more creepy, her sitting there, just watching me like that.

"You know," I said, looking up, "my name isn't Kid."

She leaned forward in her wheelchair. "What is it?" Her shoulders were sloped, but she held her chin high. Her eyes were gray but gleaming. "No, really. I want to know. You remind me of someone." Her eyes stayed glued on me, and for a second I had the sense that if she was closer, she might have reached out and touched my arm.

"Rusty," I answered. "My name's Rusty."

She nodded. "Okay. Then Rusty, will you take me sailing? Please? I'm done with work for the day. I'd love to go. I haven't been in years. By the way, *my* name is Hazel. Like the color."

Without waiting for an answer, she went right on. "See those boards over there?" She glanced toward the end of the dock and a small stack of 2 × 6 inch boards, each about four feet long, that Jack, the maintenance man at the marina, was using for repairs. "If we bring some of them over here," she said, "we can make a ramp for my wheelchair. We'll put the boards side by side. We'll set the ends of each on the edge of the dock, and the other ends in the middle of your boat. Then I'll do the rest."

She had this way of using the word *we*, as if she and I were on some team together—*her* team—and I had the feeling that she'd thought all this out before she'd even asked me. But it was totally crazy. No way was she getting into my boat.

"That's not going to work," I said. "Plus, I have to get home for supper."

"It could be a short sail. Just a half hour. Why don't we sail out to Half-tide Rock and back? The weather's perfect. It'd be grand!"

Why was she being like this? If I wasn't standing in my boat, I'd have just walked away from her. I shook my head. "No."

She gave me a long, hurt, disappointed look, as if to say, *I expected so much more of you. Where is your sense of adventure?*

At last, she seemed to give in. "Oh, well." She let out a sigh, her shoulders lifting and falling. "I tried." Then she brightened a bit. "But at least you said you'd take me *sometime*. So I suppose that could be tomorrow, or the day after, or even next week. But *sometime* we'll go sailing. Right, kid?"

So much for giving in. She turned and rolled herself back down the dock, her elbows sticking out like chicken wings, her narrow tires *thunk-thunking* over the planks. Twenty feet away, she stopped and seesawed her wheels, so that before she'd go on her way, she could peer at me over her shoulder. Her eyes twinkled in a way that held your own eyes on hers. "*Sometime*, Rusty. I'll remember that!"

CHAPTER 2

An Extra Spoon

Even when the summer people are here, life on our island is a lot slower and more old-fashioned than on the mainland, which I guess is why they all come. Fishermen still go out in wooden boats called dories. You get your hair cut at Mickey's barber shop. Some of our streets are made of cobblestones. And it's easiest to get around town by walking—or by riding your bike, which is what I was doing about a half hour after I'd finished bailing. According to the six o'clock whistle from the fire house, once again I was late for supper, not because the bailing had taken so long, but because I didn't much feel like sitting at our table. I pedaled slowly out of the marina, passed the beach, the summer people's big houses, the ferry slip, and then turned right on 3rd Street, where I came to the old bungalows like ours. I parked and trudged up the porch stairs.

“You okay, Russ?” Dad said when I came into the kitchen. In his wrinkled khaki pants and blue True Value shirt that he wears to work at the hardware store, he was already eating at the table with Lizzy. Across from her, my chair was empty, and as it’d been for exactly twenty days in a row, Mom’s chair, across from Dad, was empty too.

“I’m fine,” I said in a way that probably didn’t sound all that fine. Spaghetti and sauce were already on my plate, so I went to sit down.

“Go wash your hands,” Lizzy said, disgusted. “You’re a mess!” She had recently finished eighth grade—just three years ahead of me—but since Mom had gone, you’d have thought she was a lot older, in charge of everything, like she was running a camp.

“Take it easy,” Dad said to her and puffed out a breath. He was trying not to lose his patience. “Russ, you can warm up your food if you want.”

“If it’s cold, it serves him right!” Lizzy said, and turning to me with her dark, dagger eyes: “Can’t you tell time? Don’t they teach you that in…?” Grimacing, like she had soap in her mouth, she trailed off without adding “summer school,” while letting me know that for such a brilliant, straight-A student like herself, *summer school* was a dirty word meant for kids who *weren't too bright.* "You know, I cooked this meal, and I cooked it to be eaten on time!" she went on. "The least you could do is..."

"It's delicious," Dad cut in. "The best spaghetti I've ever had. Thanks, Lizzy. Could you pass the Parmesan cheese? Russ, go wash your hands."

At the kitchen sink, I washed my hands, while I tried not to listen to Lizzy, who kept hammering away. "So Rusty, I rang the bell, but you still didn't come, and you left your phone at home again. How are we supposed to keep track of you? You didn't set the table tonight!"

"Easy," Dad said again. "It's not a crime. Russ, you can avoid the firing squad by cleaning up after we're done. Come, have a seat. You want to warm that spaghetti?"

"No. It doesn't matter." I sat down. "Any mail today?" I tried to sound like it was no big deal.

"Nothing but bills." He shot me a glance. "Sorry about that."

For a while, Lizzy talked and talked, which is what she always does when she's riled and there's a lot of quiet to fill up. She told Dad about her day at Leadership Camp and how she was earning her Community Service badge. She told me to get my elbows off the table and not to suck my spaghetti "like a fish." Turning back to Dad, she talked about how she was voted Camper of the Week… Until Dad turned to me and asked, "So were you down at the dock this afternoon?"

This lit Lizzy's fuse again. "Of course he was!" She rolled her eyes. "Every afternoon he's either out sailing or messing around with that precious boat of his. That's all he ever does! That and read his sailing books whenever he's home."

"Lizzy," Dad said, "get off your high horse. Until you have something constructive to say, please keep your mouth shut."

"Mmmmmmm," she said, her lips clamped. She shook her head, her long black hair shivering, as if she'd been gagged—which, come to think of it, wouldn't have been a bad idea.

Ignoring her, Dad turned to me again. "Anything interesting happen today?"

Lately, he'd been trying to get me to talk more during supper, but I didn't feel like it. What could be interesting about multiplying and dividing fractions in a summer school class with four other guys slumped at their desks, all of them interested in big motor boats, and not at all interested in a boat like mine, a "dinky sailboat, that bathtub toy," they called it. And I sure wasn't going to say anything about that weird old lady and how she'd appeared out of nowhere and kept asking me to take her sailing. Lizzy would've just loved to know about that! "Nothing special," I said. "I just bailed out my boat."

"Well, at least that sounds productive," Dad said, working hard to keep the conversation upbeat. "As for me, here's some real excitement: Today I sold a toilet plunger, some shovels, and I sawed a dozen 2x4s into ten foot lengths—the Dickinsons are framing in their porch. Lizzy, do you have anything else to add about your day?"

"Mmmmmmm," she said again, meaning that bound, gagged, and forever insulted, she'd never speak with us again. "I cooked and cooked and cooked!" she said, not mentioning that she'd been at camp until about an hour before.

"I didn't realize spaghetti from a box and sauce from a jar was so complicated," Dad replied.

"I also straightened up *his* room!"

"You've got no business in there!" I said.

"Hey, you take it easy, too," Dad said to me.

Lizzy flung her hair over her shoulder and kept talking to Dad like I didn't exist. "His room, it was a disaster area! His clothes were all over the place. Same with his stupid sailing books."

"You keep your hands off those!" I yelled.

"You didn't have to do all that," Dad said to her sharply.

"Well, who else was gonna straighten his room? Or *make* him do it?"

We all got quiet now. Suddenly I could see Mom walking into my room in her sandals, jeans, and a loose sweater with the sleeves pushed up her narrow arms to her elbows. She'd look around the room calmly and nod, as if there was something she didn't like but understood. She wouldn't be mad. She might even give me her soft, teasing smile. *I'll bet you an extra dollar allowance that I can finish the dishes before you've cleaned up this place.* Before I could answer, down to the kitchen she'd go, her sandals clicking on the stairs.

In silence, we finished our spaghetti. Then, clearing the table, Dad said, "Hey, I brought home some ice cream for dessert! Mint chocolate chip. Three bowls coming up! And chocolate sauce all around! Russ, would you get some spoons?"

I went to the drawer and, without thinking, grabbed four spoons to put around the table. As I was putting down the fourth at Mom's usual place, I stopped, took it back, but not before Lizzy saw me.

"What's wrong with you?!" she screamed, so furious that I thought she might explode. "Why do you keep doing these things? Can't you get it through your thick head? Don't you understand? SHE… ISN'T… HERE!"

"I KNOW THAT!" I screamed back at her. "DO YOU THINK I'M BLIND!? LEAVE ME ALONE!!"

Dad put his hands out in front of him, sort of patting the air in a steadying way. "Let's everybody take a step back. Hang on. We're all in the same boat here, for goodness sakes."

I slammed the spoon back in the drawer.

Where Mom *was*, as Dad had told us, was at some place called Woodhaven, where she was supposed to be getting better. Neither Lizzy nor I had been there—it was over two hundred miles beyond the ferry pier on the mainland. It was supposed to have fields and woods around it, with walking paths, a stable of horses, and a clinic with nice nurses and doctors. "A place for healing," Dad had called it.

But why exactly did Mom need healing? What was she healing *from*? How long would she be there? Why couldn't we see her? Why was only Dad allowed to call her, and only once a week? Why were Lizzy and I only allowed to write her letters? I'd written three of them in pen on special paper that Dad had given us. But she hadn't answered.

Why? And why had she gotten sick, or whatever it was, in the first place?

"Come. Sit down. Have some ice cream," Dad said in that way of his, as if he knew exactly what kept pounding and pounding in my head.

CHAPTER 3

Mom

At first Lizzy and me, we thought it was just a bad cold. This was in early May, about a year ago. Mom's voice was husky. She seemed drowsy. And when I came home from school in the afternoons, she'd still be in her pink nightgown, waiting in the kitchen. As usual, I'd make myself some toast with honey, and Mom would slowly fix herself a cup of cinnamon tea. I loved that time, before Lizzy and Dad came home. We'd sit at the table, and after she breathed in the steam rising from her cup, Mom would lean forward with her wavy hair brushing her shoulders, her chin in her hand, and look at me with her brown eyes that still were deep and warm. "So how did things go today?"

And I'd tell her, even if things, like math, didn't go so well.

But then came an afternoon when Mom was in

her bedroom when I came home. I went upstairs and knocked softly on the door. There was a pause, like she was waking up. Through the door, I asked, "You okay? Are you sick?"

Her voice came almost word by word. "No… I'm… not sick"

"Can I make you a cup of tea?"

"That's nice. No. Thanks. I'll… be out… soon."

Eventually, when she did come out, she was still in her nightgown, but with her arms hanging down like long sticks, her hair messy, her eyes dark and hollow, and her voice so flat and weak that I could hardly hear it. She blinked and then said as if she was surprised and confused, "Oh. Rusty. It's you. Home? From school? Already?"

In the week after that, she sometimes came out of her room, but sometimes didn't, and I ate my snack by myself. That was when Dad talked with Dr. Murphy on his phone and took Mom to the Island Medical Center, where she got some medicine. That was also when I started watering Mom's garden because she seemed to have forgotten about it. And that was when Lizzy started cooking suppers—another thing Mom seemed to have forgotten. When he'd get home from work, Dad would go upstairs to their bedroom and shut the door. Lizzy and I would hear them talking up there, mostly Dad talking softly. Eventually, both of them would come slowly downstairs, and Dad, making a tight-lipped smile, would be holding Mom's hand. She'd be dressed, but her shirttails might not be tucked in straight and her hair would hang like seaweed. She seemed to shuffle more than walk, like someone moving in shoes without any laces. And here was the worst thing of all: She couldn't look into our eyes.

Slouched at the table, she barely ate or said a word. And then one evening in the middle of June, as we were finishing our macaroni and cheese that Lizzy had made, Mom dropped her fork, put her face in her hands, and just started sobbing. "I'm sorry. I'm sorry," was all she said, as Dad, with his hand around her waist, helped her back up to their bedroom, where he stayed the rest of that evening and night—the first night I'd ever gone to bed without someone saying goodnight.

The next day, Dad didn't go to work at all, and when I came home from school, I could hear him on his phone in their bedroom, with the door closed and his voice low. There were words that I understood and others that I didn't: "Residential treatment and therapy." "So far away?" "How long?" "How much?" "A loan?" "Remortgage the house." "Of course we'll do what we have to."

"What's wrong with Mom?" I asked that night when I was in bed and he came into my room.

He sat on the edge of the bed, like he did when I was younger. "I'm not sure." His voice was tired. "I think she's very sad."

"Why?"

"I'm not sure," he said again.

"Is this what happened to Jimmy Dawes's dad?" Jimmy was a kid in my grade, whose father went away on a trip and never came back, except once to get his clothes.

"No," Dad said. "It's nothing like that."

"Was it something I did? Or Lizzy?"

He leaned over and put his arms around me, so tight that I could smell the hardware store, that sawdust smell, in the folds of his shirt. "No," he said. "Don't even think that. It's not because of either of you guys. That I'm sure of. Believe me."

Through the open window beside my bed, I could hear the *hush-hush* of lapping waves, like the sound you hear inside a seashell, which is really the beat of your own heart. "What's going to happen?"

"We're going to try to make things better, get some more help. Doctor Murphy said Mom needs special doctors. So I've made an appointment over on the mainland. I'm going to take her there early in the morning."

"Can we come, Lizzy and me?"

"Probably not. It's far away. Besides, it's a school day for you."

"When will you be back?"

"Tomorrow evening."

"Will Mom be with you?"

He let out a long breath and ran his hand through his sandy hair. "I'm not sure. She may need to stay there a while. But in time things should get better." He looked at me closely. "Okay?"

When he left, I heard the lapping waves again, and tried to keep my mind on them. Out at the marina, there'd be lots of sailboats, some tied in slips and others moored in the moonlit water. It'd look like a forest of masts sticking up, with lines, or ropes, crisscrossing the sky and silver-blue light on the decks and railings. The sails would be rolled up tight. The breeze would be warm, the water covered in dimples. The halyards, the lines that raise the sails, would *clink-clink* against the masts. And that soft, slow rocking, rocking...

The next morning, Dad led Mom down the stairs, while Lizzy and I ate our cereal in the kitchen. He was carrying Mom's small, black suitcase, and she was wearing her gray pants and a sweater with the buttons in the wrong holes. She looked thin. The pants hung loosely around her hips, and she moved like she might break. From the hall closet, Dad got her raincoat and put it over her shoulders. I hadn't even noticed it was raining. "I'll be back for supper," he said. "Make sure the door is shut when you leave for school. Come give Mom a kiss."

She bent toward us. We kissed her, but she didn't seem to see us. She seemed to be half-asleep. Then together they turned toward the front door, Dad with a pale look on his face, the suitcase in one hand, and his other holding Mom's elbow. The screen door *screeeked* and smacked. Their slow steps went down the porch stairs, and soon we heard the car doors open and close.

For some reason, Lizzy and I didn't, or couldn't, get up from the table. We seemed to be watching a movie at the same time that we were *in* it, and the movie just kept going and going. I wanted to run down to the car and yell "Stop!" I wanted to beat on the car window. I wanted the movie to go in reverse and for Mom and Dad to walk back up the stairs and into the kitchen, where Dad would put down the suitcase. But all Lizzy and I could do was look at our cereal bowls, at the two empty chairs on either end of the table, at the stove and the door, while we listened to the car start, shift into forward, and the windshield wipers slap. We heard the car pull away, turn down 3rd Street, the *shishing* sound of tires on wet pavement, and then all those sounds were gone. Ten minutes later, it was our turn to move. We didn't look at each other. We put on raincoats and threw our backpacks over our shoulders, as the long, low blast of the ferry horn echoed and echoed. It was the 7:15, the first ferry of the day, heading off toward the mainland. We shut the door behind us and walked toward school. That's when Lizzy, my evil sister, grabbed my hand and held it tight, and I didn't even try to pull it away.

• • •

After supper, Dad came home with just his keys in his hand and his eyes very sad. "She's going to be okay," he said to me and Lizzy, trying to reassure us, but none of us slept well that night. In fact, sometime after 2 a.m., I got a strange scary taste, like metal, in my mouth, and I couldn't stop my legs and arms from shaking. I got up and opened the little door to the storage area behind the low wall on one side of my room. I crawled in and curled up in the piles of folded winter clothes, the knitted hats, scarves, and sweaters. Some of them were Mom's and smelled like her—a little like Ivory soap, a little like her tea.

And that's where I found myself, right there in the storage area, when I woke up the next morning. Dad was on his knees peering in at me. "Russ, what in the world are you doing in there?"

"I don't know," I said.

But I think he knew. Because when he came home that evening, he came straight to the work shed in our backyard, where I was putting off my homework and avoiding the kids at the park who already were saying, "Hey, my dad saw your mom on the ferry. She going nuts?" I was nailing pieces of scrap wood together for no particular reason, except that I wanted to hammer something. *Bam! Bam-Bam!*

Dad shut the double doors behind him. He was tired from his day's work and everything else. In his quiet way, he came up alongside me at the workbench and put his hand on my shoulder. I stopped hammering. He asked me if those were 12 penny nails, and he asked me about my day at school. "Anything new?"

"Not much." At the moment, school and all the end-of-year tests were the farthest things from my mind.

Then out of the blue, he said, "I had an interesting conversation today with Mr. Clark, who came into the store to buy a sprinkler. He asked how we were

doing and, because he's a neighbor, I went ahead and told him that we were having a tough time. He said he was sorry. And then it occurred to me to ask if he had any plans for that sailboat of his, you know, the one that's been lying in the ivy behind his house for a couple of years. He said no, that actually he'd forgotten all about it. So I mentioned that I knew someone who might be interested in it, and I think he figured out what I was driving at, because the next thing he said was, 'Hey, I've got an idea. If Rusty wants to fix up the boat, and if he'll take good care of it, well, I'd like him to have it. And sail it. He can keep it if he wants. I'd rather see that boat right side up in the water than upside down in my yard.'" Dad rubbed his jaw with his hand. "So what do you think, Russ?"

I thought of all the boats I'd seen but never set foot on. Mostly they were the summer people's boats: the ones in their private slips, the ones racing, impossibly tilted way out on the bay, and the ones drifting around their mooring buoys.

"I've never fixed up a boat before," I said. "I don't know how to sail either."

"Well, you could learn," Dad said. "You're old enough. You could start by reading some books. It might be a good thing to try."

CHAPTER 4

Meeting on Bayshore Street

In case you don't know, summer school is one of the worst things ever invented. It's torture. Not only does everyone think you're stupid, and not only do you have to spend your weekday mornings at school, but you have to do it after your classmates have cleaned out their lockers and said "Have a great summer! See you in sixth grade!" and when everyone else is on vacation, or at camp, or just hanging out. Outside the classroom windows, I could see kids playing softball, running around with their shirts off. I could hear them yelling, "safe!" or "out!" or "I've got it!" while right in front of me and those four other guys, Mrs. Kaminski was scribbling numbers on the board, with the skin on her upper arm wobbling like Jell-O.

Anyways, three or four days after I saw that old lady Hazel on the dock, I was walking home alone from school, and you might imagine how lousy I felt. Lizzy was at camp. I had a long homework assignment, and I'd just called to check in with Dad, who as usual was too busy at work to come home for lunch. Sometimes I'd stop by my friend Walter's house, where his mom would make us grilled cheese sandwiches, and then we'd play his video games or ping-pong in his garage, or go down to the dock to do some things on my boat. Each of us is the sort of friend you have when you don't have other friends. Right above his forehead, Walter has a cowlick that makes his hair look funny, and he's as skinny as me—and even shorter. We steer clear of the kids who are good at sports. We're in the same grade. We've stuck together. But two days before, I'd gotten mad at him for tracking mud into my boat. He'd gone home all ticked off, calling me "crabby and cranky." Then he went off to sleep-away camp in Vermont for six weeks, and now it seemed like I was the only person left in the world. I was going home to make myself a sandwich and see what was on TV.

But as I turned onto Bayshore Street around a high stone wall, I practically collided with Hazel, who was coming around the corner in her wheelchair. If I'd known she was coming before she saw me, I would have turned down a side street. Instead, we both stopped. She was wearing those same rubber-soled shoes, but with brown pants and a loose, cream-colored shirt with a collar. Her hair was neatly combed and pulled into a bun on the back of her head, and she had a watermelon strapped on her lap with her seat belt.

"Hey kid!" she said. "What a surprise! What's up? Where are you going?"

It occurred to me to say *None of your business*, but it's hard to say that to someone in a wheelchair, even if it's someone like Hazel. "Home. For lunch," I said and started walking again in that direction.

"Wait! So am I! Why don't you come along? How does egg salad sound? And here's dessert!" She pointed to the watermelon. "I can't eat this all by myself."

The watermelon made me pause, but then I kept walking.

"Hold on, Rusty!" She was speaking quickly now, her words tumbling out and running all together: "Look, I'm sorry about the other day. I got carried away. I just saw you in your boat, and I had a picture that I couldn't get out of my head. I wanted to go sailing again. Just one more time..."

I stopped about twenty feet away and turned to face her. She'd moved her wheels to keep me in view.

"... But I had no business badgering you like that," she went on. "It's your boat to do anything you want with. What was I thinking? I'm sorry. I really am."

Now she came halfway toward me, stopped, and said as if it was some fancy invitation, "Will you join me for lunch?" Then she added, "I won't ask again, even if you say no. I promise." Her eyes were pouched. Her ankles and shins, in thick, flesh-colored stockings, looked as skinny as pencils. Brown spots, like the ones on old bananas, speckled her knobby hands, which seemed for an instant to shake. She was an old lady in a wheelchair with a watermelon in her lap. There was something at once funny, serious, and sad about her that kept me from turning and leaving. What was I afraid of? Without Walter around, I really didn't have anything else going on that afternoon. Besides, I love watermelon. And to be honest, I'd been wondering about Hazel, like something I couldn't get out of my head—or like a pebble stuck in my sneaker. Where exactly did she live? *How* did she live? And why did she seem so interested in me?

"All right," I said. Why not?

"Thanks," she replied, more relieved than you'd expect. "My cottage is a little ways down the street here. Where are you coming from?"

I figured I couldn't keep this from her much longer. After all, I had my pack, with my huge textbook, on my back. So I decided to get it over with: "School," I said.

She thought for a second, putting two and two together. "Hmm. That would mean *summer* school. Let me guess. Math?"

I nodded, then looked away down the street.

I expected her to say something that other people always say, like *Sorry to hear that* or *That's too bad*, but she didn't say anything more about it. She just seemed to be thinking.

With that over, we turned around, away from the village center, and I walked slowly beside and a half step behind her, as she pushed the rims of her wheels. I wondered about asking if she'd like me to carry the watermelon, but there was a message in the way that she held her chin high and moved steadily down the street: *I can manage on my own, thank you very much!*

We came to a crosswalk. "We take a left here," she said.

CHAPTER 5
The Cottage

Oak Lane is a narrow, dead-end street, where the pavement is bumpy and the sidewalk disappears. On either side are some woods and a few beat-up looking houses, with peeling paint, that are even smaller than ours. Hazel pointed out the trees beside the street—the oaks, maples, and chestnuts—and told me how you can tell the difference between them, not just by their leaves, but by the pattern of their branches, the shape, size, and color of their twigs, and by their barks, whether they're smooth, rough, cracked, or flaking.

"How do you know all these things?" I asked.

"Well, you just have to look. Closely, that is. And besides, my name is Hazel, and a hazel is a kind of bushy tree—not just a color. Hazels have smooth bark. The seeds are nuts that you can eat. You've heard of hazelnuts, right? Long, long ago, the Celts, who lived in Europe, thought they gave you wisdom. And the leaves have sharp, prickly edges…" She gave me one of her amused glances. "… *just like me.*"

I couldn't see any houses at the end of the street, just some dark woods that didn't look too inviting. "Your house is down *here*?" I asked. This was one of those out-of-the-way places on the island that most people don't know about, or try to avoid.

"Yup," she said. "We'll be there soon." She steered toward a weedy, crumbling brick path that you wouldn't notice unless you were looking for it. It was so narrow that I had to follow her, single file, as it wound slightly uphill and deeper into the thick bushes and trees.

What am I getting into? I thought as I asked aloud, "How do you do this when there's snow?"

Hazel pushed a branch out of her way. "Oh, I have someone shovel me out and put down salt. No problem. It's not like I'm in the middle of nowhere."

At a wooden gate, she picked up a stick leaning on the gatepost and with it lifted the latch. Then she pushed the gate open with the footrest of her wheelchair and rolled through. Up ahead, in a small, overgrown yard, I could see her cottage. It could have come from a fairy tale. Long ago, it'd been the gardener's house on a big farm that "had fallen on hard times," Hazel said as we passed a tree with little blossoms on it. The cottage was one story, with a mossy slate roof, a tilted stone chimney on one end, and shaggy shingles, some hanging cockeyed like bad teeth. Two tiny windows, each with a box of yellow flowers beneath it, peered out of the front. Between them was a chipped blue door, and on an upturned log beside the door sat a wooden mailbox shaped and painted like a seagull sitting in water. By pulling down its head and beak, Hazel opened the box and took out a newspaper and a few letters. Then she lifted the mailbox and from beneath it, slid out a key to let us into the cottage.

In the moment it took for my eyes to adjust to the darker light inside, something rubbed against my shin and made me shiver.

"Hello, Marigold!" Hazel said.

A yellow and brown cat with white mitten paws and fur so fluffy it look electrified came into focus. She must have liked my leg.

"Well, you seem to have found a friend," Hazel said.

We were in her living room, or at least that's where I thought we were. It was hard to tell because it was so full. On the floor stood teetering stacks of books and magazines. A tower of *National Geographic* magazines came up to my waist. Other stacks included file folders, encyclopedias, and old record albums. A number of big clay pots occupied one corner, each sprouting with tall, dried grasses and giant feathers. Near a doorway was a wooden statue with faces carved into it, like part of a totem pole. And the walls? Well, you couldn't see them. They were either lined with bookcases crammed with books, shells, pottery, dried seaweed, lacy snake skins, birds' nests, dusty carvings of gulls, a pair of binoculars, a wooden yo-yo, an old brass pocket compass with a lid, and an entire standing skeleton of what might have been a fox… Or they were covered with postcards, framed paintings, photographs, and maps of just about everywhere, including places like China and Antarctica, which got me thinking about the great explorers, who, of course, were sailors.

"Cool!" I said under my breath.

The room was like a little museum that could have used Lizzy's cleaning and organizing, except that it seemed more interesting just as it was. There was no TV. No sofa. No coffee table. No computer. On a desk was an ancient record player, and near the fireplace stood a worn armchair with a newspaper open to the crossword puzzle and a book tented on the seat. So yes, I guess it *was* a living room, but for a different kind of living than I was used to.

While I was looking around, Hazel closed the front door. "Home sweet home," she said. "As you can see, it can use some tidying up, but I never seem to get around to it." She glanced through her mail, then unhooked the seatbelt around the watermelon. "Now you *can* do me a favor," she said, as if she'd read my mind when we'd started walking here. "Could you carry this into the kitchen? Just take it straight back through that doorway and across the hall."

I took the watermelon and put it on the counter in the kitchen, which was pretty much a regular old kitchen: a sink, a refrigerator, a toaster, an old telephone on the wall with a stretchy spiral cord, a couple of bowls in the corner for Marigold, and beneath an open window, a small wooden table with a brass lamp made from a candle holder.

When I came back into the living room, following a path between the stacks of magazines and folders, I was surprised to see Hazel standing. She had one hand on a handle of her wheelchair and the other holding a wooden cane. She might have been about as tall as me, if she wasn't bent forward at her waist, and if her shoulders weren't so hunched. Still, she held the cane straight out toward me, like she was sword fighting.

"On guard!" she said, with a big smile on her face.

"You can stand!" I said.

"Of course! And with my helper here"—she rapped her cane on the planked floor—"I can get around the house just fine. If I put my mind to it, I can still do a lot of things," she said, not bragging, but in that plain way of hers. "So much in life just depends on putting your mind to it. Not everything, of course, but probably more than you think." She waved the cane at me again. "Would you mind stepping out of my way?"

CHAPTER 6

Milk (sort of) and a Sandwich

Favoring her right leg, which seemed stiffer than the other, Hazel hobbled away from her wheelchair, through the doorway, and across the hall, her cane tapping with each step. When she could, she put her free hand on the wall or a doorknob to steady herself, and in this way she got around pretty well but slowly, like she was wading through thick mud that I couldn't see. I followed her into the kitchen. Leaning awkwardly, she poured dried food into one cat bowl. The other was half full of milk.

Turning to me, she said, "So it's egg salad, right?"

"Yes. Please." Without thinking about it, I was using what my mom called "manners." I hung my backpack over a chair.

Hazel opened the refrigerator and pulled out a head of lettuce, a loaf of bread, and a container of egg salad. "Do you like bread or toast?"

"Toast. Thanks."

"That's my favorite, too."

The refrigerator door was covered with photos stuck on with little magnets.

"That top one there is my daughter, Ann, when she graduated from college twenty-five years ago," Hazel said, dropping slices of bread into the toaster. "She's an accountant in Phoenix. Very busy." The next photo was of a friendly-looking old man in a straw hat. "That's Malcolm, my late husband. And by 'late' I don't mean that he was never on time."

"I know what 'late' means," I said. *It means he died*, I said to myself. I bent toward another photo of a younger man with narrow shoulders in a wrinkled coat and tie, and with a girl in pigtails standing beside him.

"That's my son, Charlie," Hazel went on. "And he *is* the one who's always late. He was late getting himself born and late all the time for the school bus. He was even late for his own wedding and late for Emily's birth—she's the girl, my granddaughter, there. Cute as a button. They all live on the west coast, in Oregon, so I don't see much of them."

For a moment, she seemed lost in her thoughts, as

she spread egg salad on slices of toast.

"Do you have friends?" I asked, surprised that the question popped out of me.

"They're almost all gone. I see lots of people at the Art Barn, but I can't really call them friends." After a pause, she said, "Truth is, I don't get along so well with most people my age." She laughed, then shook her head. "They're all so *old!* And the ones I know complain too much. They seem too scared to live, I mean *really* live. I guess I rile them up. They say I don't 'act my age.' They always want to 'fix' me. Milk?"

From a cupboard, she got two glasses and, to my surprise, took a red and white box, the size of a cereal box, from the cupboard. "Carnation Powdered Milk," I read. She shook some white stuff into the glasses, added water, and stirred it. "Real milk goes bad too fast. I prefer this," she said. She handed me a clean, plaid napkin, and we sat on either side of the little table.

The sandwich was good, but the powdered milk was the worst thing I'd ever tasted, like liquid chalk. It was horrible. It didn't seem to bother Hazel, though. Nor did the horrible face I made.

"More milk?" she asked with that amused look coming back to her. "Marigold loves it, too."

"No," I managed to say. "Thanks."

For a time, then, we ate without speaking, like we were being cautious, waiting for each other to say something, and I wondered what Mom might think of Hazel, if she'd known her better. You can't imagine two more different people, Mom so calm and quiet, and Hazel so... *out there*, I guess you could say. But I think Mom would have liked her. And maybe vice versa. *A real character*, is what Mom might have called her. *Her very own person.*

Meanwhile, Marigold jumped up in my lap and purred like a motor. A midday breeze, smelling like pines warmed by the sun, came in through the open window. Beyond the window, I could see a small brick patio with a couple of green plastic chairs, a side table, some potted herbs, a bird feeder on a tall pole, and beyond that the woods.

"Believe me, I'm not asking you again to take me sailing, but could you tell me about that boat of yours?" Hazel finally said, like she'd been wondering about it a while. "I've never seen a catboat without a centerboard. It must have a fixed keel, right?"

I was impressed that she'd noticed this, so I told her how Mr. Clark had modified it, and how for years it'd been upside down in his yard, with the mast and sail stowed beneath it. Each winter, snow mounded over it, and in the summers ivy crisscrossed it, until you couldn't tell if it was there at all, except for the keel sticking up like a fin. I told her how Mr. Clark had said I could have it, and how Dad and I had hacked away the ivy and carried the hull to our work shed and set it on sawhorses. Then I told her that I'd worked on it every day after school for weeks. Scraping. Sanding. Caulking. Varnishing. Polishing all the brass. When he had time, Dad would help, and so would my friend Walter, even though he never went sailing because it made him sick. "Then one day—it was the Saturday after school ended—Dad, Mr. Clark, Walter, and me carried the boat all the way to the beach, waded in, and put it in the water. It didn't leak a drop!"

"Wonderful!" Hazel said, and I could tell she understood. Something about boats made both of us happy.

So I kept going. I'm not usually a talker—that's Lizzy's department—but the words kept coming. "The next afternoon, Mr. Clark helped me attach the rudder to the transom on the back of the boat. I got the mast up and rigged the sail—that's very complicated, you know. Then I organized everything else that Mr. Clark had given me—the anchor, extra lines, life jackets, foot straps, tool box, first aid kit—all in the compartments under the seats. Everything has its special place on a catboat."

"Ship shape!" Hazel said. "And since then, you've learned to sail?"

"Well, I'm learning. I'm not very good. I can do some things in an easy breeze. Usually I can tack—that's when you turn your boat to go across the wind. And I can come into the dock on the leeward side—that's the downwind side..."

Hazel seemed to smile to herself. "I think I've heard those words," she said gently.

"... And I have some sailing books that I bought," I went on. "They have pictures, directions, checklists, and quizzes you can take. And I've been practicing out on the water most afternoons!"

"Amazing! You must be determined!" She paused, thinking. "But why, after all those years, did Mr. Clark give you the boat *now*?"

I didn't want to say, *Because he felt sorry for me*, so I took another bite of my sandwich.

Hazel's eyebrows knit together, and then after a moment, leaning forward with her elbow on the table, she asked, "Did this have something to do with your mom?"

I nodded.

"I see," she said, looking me in the eye. And it seemed that, just as she knew about trees and boats, she knew something about this sort of thing, as well. "Will she be home soon?"

"I don't know."

"I hope so."

For a time, we were silent again, and when Hazel had finished her sandwich, she picked up a small rectangular plastic container from beside the lamp. It had seven square sections in it, all lined up in a row, and from the one labeled "Tues" she took three pills, one red, one white, and a brown one shaped like a football. She swallowed each with a quick gulp of milk.

"What are those for?" It was odd, but I felt like I could ask her anything.

"Oh, they're for my creaky joints, and a few other things. Can I make you another sandwich?"

I said no, I was leaving room for watermelon.

"Well, before we have dessert," she said, "we both have some work to do."

I stared at her.

"I bet you have math homework. Right?"

I could see where *this* was going, and I wasn't crazy

about its direction.

"Why don't you get started on it for twenty minutes," she said, "while I do some work of my own." It was more of a statement than a question. In fact, there was *no* question about it at all. "*Then* we'll have watermelon," she added.

She pushed herself up and out of her chair. "Clear your place so you can work here." She hobbled into the living room and put a record on her record player. I heard scratching and drums and trumpets. Then I heard her cane tapping along the hallway and into a room down there.

I set Marigold on the floor and put my dish in the sink.

"Have you started your math?" she called over the music.

"Not yet."

"Well, our twenty minutes begin as soon as you get started. Let me know."

I pulled my math textbook from my backpack and looked at today's assignment: converting fractions into decimals and rounding to the nearest hundredth. What a pain. As always, the book was heavy as bricks. What a waste of ink and trees. When

I opened it, it gave off a faint smell, like onions, that made my eyes water. "I'm starting now," I called, and began with the first problem, dividing the numerator by the denominator.

CHAPTER 7

Spitting Seeds

Exactly twenty minutes later, according to the clock on the stove, I heard Hazel's cane tapping in the hall. "Isn't that stirring!" she said, referring to the music that reached its very loud ending as she came into the kitchen. "Makes me want to climb a mountain!" At the kitchen counter, she began slicing the watermelon on a cutting board. "You make any progress on your math?"

"A little."

I thought she might ask me to show her my homework, but she said, "Good. Finish it at home tonight. Then double check your answers. Let's take these out on the patio. Bring your napkin. Marigold stays inside." Hazel handed me two plates, each with a fork and a thick wedge of watermelon, and we passed through a tiny room that she called a "mud room," where she kept Marigold's litter box. Then we went out the back door and sat side by side in the green chairs, Hazel's cane hanging over the arm of hers, and our plates balanced on our laps.

I'd never eaten watermelon with a fork, and each time I stabbed into my wedge, a bite-sized piece shot off my plate and onto my shorts.

Hazel considered this. "Well, I guess we aren't at the Plaza." Then, giving me a wink, she said, "The heck with these forks," and picking up her watermelon in both hands, she went at it, teeth first.

I followed her lead. Isn't that how you're supposed to eat watermelon? And if you're like me, when you take your first big bite, you forget all about… the seeds. What do you do with them? Lizzy, never wanting to make a mess, actually swallows the seeds, and I've seen Mom neatly drop them one by one from her lips to a spoon, and then put them in a line on the edge of a paper plate.

I figured Hazel might do something like that, but no. Her face got all serious and not-serious at once. She took in a deep breath through her nose, slowly pulled her head back, and then, in the instant of snapping it forward and making a sharp sound like *ppphaah!*, she spat out a seed, shooting it across the patio, over a potted geranium, and into the grass near the woods.

"Whoa!" I'd never seen anybody but kids spit watermelon seeds.

She nodded at me, her eyes twinkling: my turn. So I chewed more watermelon, curled my tongue like a tube around a seed, and spat it, bazooka-style, as far as I could. It landed a little closer to the woods than Hazel's. I raised my arms in victory. "Yes!!!"

But then she, after another bite and gathering herself like a shot-putter, breathed in even more deeply, puffed out her cheeks like a hamster, and launched another seed farther yet. You'd never guess she had so much breath! The seed dinged off the metal squirrel baffle beneath the bird feeder. "A new world record!" she said, with red juice on her cheeks and arms. "Bet you can't beat that?"

"Oh yeah?"

Then back and forth we went, biting in, chewing, slurping, loading, aiming, cocking our heads, and firing. It was fun. It was a mess. We laughed. And as we went on, there was something else to it, something that somehow seemed important, as if we *needed* to do this. So we just kept going and going, spitting farther and farther, with all our might, like there were things inside us that we had to get out, like we were spitting more than seeds.

Eventually, we chewed down to the hard, green rinds. Hazel looked at her watch. “Time to go,” she said, grabbing her cane. “Time to get back to the Art Barn.”

We took our plates and rinds into the kitchen and left. At the end of her street, near that high stone wall, we turned to go our separate ways. “You can stop by the cottage any day for lunch,” Hazel said before wheeling off. “See you.”

CHAPTER 8

Some Calculations

For the rest of that afternoon and evening, I couldn't stop thinking how both strange and ordinary it'd felt to be at Hazel's cottage. Strange because I'd never been to a place like that with a person like that, and ordinary because it actually seemed pretty normal to be there with her. I wondered what Walter would think about this. Some kids, I knew, called Hazel a "crazy old lady." But was she crazy? Or was I crazy for even going there?

Over the next two days, I didn't stop at Hazel's. From summer school, I went straight home for lunch and watered Mom's garden. Then I rode down to the dock and took my boat out on the water, never far from the marina, and practiced tacking: pushing the tiller (a long handle which operates the rudder) toward the sail, crossing to the other side of the boat as it crosses the wind, and trimming (adjusting) the sail to the new tack (a new direction). I didn't see Hazel at all.

So there might not have been any more to this story, if Dad, when he'd come into my room to say good night on the next Saturday, hadn't told me about something on his mind. I was in bed looking through my sailing books and trying not to think too much about Mom. I'd been imagining myself, just like in the pictures, sailing across the bay, or gliding back into the marina, the sail gently flapping, slowing us down, the boat coming to rest beside the dock, where I'd step off with the bow line in my hand, as easy as stepping into a room.

Hands in pockets, Dad leaned back against my desk. He looked uncertain and even more tired than normal, I guess because Lizzy had been chewing him out for not doing the laundry again. I put down the yard-long length of rope that I had in one hand and put my finger in the page of the book I was reading —instructions for tying some fancy knots. As usual, Dad wore his wrinkled khakis and True Value shirt. He came over and picked up the end of the rope and looked at the two half hitches I'd made around the bedpost. He gave it a little tug. "Nice," he said. "That'll hold... unlike the Red Sox relief pitching lately." Then he seemed to weigh whether he should say something else or not. Finally, he said, "Guess what."

I perked up, thinking he might have some news about Mom.

"You know that funny old woman, Hazel, who sells paintings in that little garage in town?"

I didn't say yes or no.

"Well, this afternoon at work, she came through the door in her wheelchair, rolled right up to me like she owned the place and asked, 'Would your son like a summer job?' Never mind that I was trying to help another customer at the time. When I said, 'I'll be right with you,' she didn't seem to hear. She kept right on talking. 'I believe his name is Rusty,' she said. 'I saw him some days ago on the dock, and it occurs to me that he might like a small but steady job for the rest of the summer.' Russ, do you know this old lady?"

That was Hazel all right, and I said yes, I knew who she was. But feeling so strange about her, I didn't say *how* I knew her, or how well.

"Anyways, she says she has some jobs to do around her house. Cleaning up, cutting grass, washing windows—that sort of thing. You'd work three afternoons a week, her afternoons off, and she'd pay five dollars an hour. If you'd like to do it, she said you should drop by her shop—you know, the Art Barn—

or her home. She said she lives on Oak Lane." Dad shook his head and his eyebrows went up. "Then she turned on a dime and rolled straight out the door. She wasn't much interested in hardware."

Right off, I didn't know what to think about this.

"If you're interested," Dad said, "you might talk with her first to make sure you'll get along with each other—she's a piece of work, that lady. On the other hand, you *do* have all your afternoons free, and I bet you could find some use for the money. Whatever you decide is all right with me. It's your call."

Pretty accurately, Dad had described what was ping ponging back and forth in my brain. What would it be like to work for Hazel? She was so weird. Would the money be worth it?

After Dad had gone across the hall into Lizzy's room to say goodnight, I did some math calculations, something I didn't usually do for the heck of it.

In my head, I figured that at five dollars an hour, I'd have to work three hours to buy that $14.55 wind indicator that Buddy D sold at The Dock Shop. This meant that after working *only one afternoon*, I could have it, that arrow-shaped indicator for the top of my mast, a kind of special weather vane that spins in any direction and always points into the wind!

Then I made a bigger calculation, which I did with a pencil on a page of one of my sailing books. I wrote $110.95, an unbelievable amount of money, as the numerator. I divided by five, and found that after twenty-three more hours of work, I could buy a round mooring buoy with a bright blue stripe, so I wouldn't have to tie my boat to the dock like a dinghy. Instead, I could moor it a little ways out in the bay, where it would swing around with the changing wind, the sun winking on its polished wood and chrome, as bright and proud as the summer people's big sailboats.

CHAPTER 9
A Job

So the next day, I went from school to Hazel's cottage. When I walked up to it, the front door was partway open, and although she couldn't see me and I hadn't even knocked yet, Hazel's raspy voice called out over her music, "Rusty, come on in!"

She was sitting in the armchair beside the fireplace, her white hair lit up beneath the standing lamp. She was wearing those round glasses that you see on grouchy librarians, and it hit me that maybe this wasn't the best idea, coming here again, even if I might get a job out of it.

"Welcome. Give me a couple minutes," she said, turning a page of her book. "Make yourself at home."

I put down my backpack, took a magazine off the stack of *National Geographics*, and sat cross-legged on a patch of floor that wasn't covered in books or magazines. Marigold, purring and tickling me with her long whiskers, slid in and out of my arms, so I had to lift up the magazine to read about some amazing birds, called chimney swifts, that fly from caves in South America to their summer homes in chimneys as far away as Canada.

"Lunch is on," Hazel said in a while, closing her book and leaving her glasses on the arm of the chair. "Come whenever you're ready. Tuna sandwiches." She got up and with her cane hobbled into the kitchen while I followed. She was wearing an olive green dress without a belt and with little yellow flowers printed on it.

"Read anything interesting?" she asked.

I told her about the chimney swifts.

"Fascinating!" *Fascinating* was one of her favorite words. She liked to be fascinated. "Rusty, if you don't turn out to be a sailor, you could be an ornithologist and study birds." Something else clicked in her mind, and then something else again: "Or maybe you could be an astronomer! Sailors used to sail by the stars."

On either side of the table, two sandwiches were already on separate plates. One plate was beside a glass of powdered milk, the other beside a glass of water. Next to the glass of water lay the same plaid napkin Hazel had given me the other day, only now it'd been pulled through a shiny, stainless steel shackle, U-shaped with a bolt across the open end, which you use to connect lines to sails on boats.

"A shackle!" I said.

"I thought you'd like it." She looked very pleased. "A perfect napkin ring. I bought it at The Dock Shop yesterday."

"How did you know I was coming?"

"I didn't… But I had a feeling."

And I also had a feeling: that she was watching me out of the corner of her eye, as if to figure out how I was doing. We sat. I pulled my napkin out through the shackle—I noticed that her napkin ring was a simple wooden O—and we started eating.

"So what's on your mind?" she said, though I'm sure she already knew.

"My Dad said you had some work for me, if I wanted to do it."

"Well?"

"Well…" I swallowed down what was in my mouth. "I think I'd like to."

Hazel put down her sandwich and actually pumped her fist in the air. "Terrific! I have the afternoon off. So why not start right away?" Then she paused. "After you've done some homework."

• • •

My first job, after twenty minutes of math and after we'd had some sliced peaches, was to cut down the tall weeds and grasses that had made Hazel's little front yard look like a hayfield. I used what she called a "scythe," an L-shaped tool with a long shaft and a foot-long, double-sided blade at the bottom that you swing back and forth like a golf club, chopping off the grass near the ground. It took me a while to get the hang of it, but eventually I did, more or less. You just wade in and start swinging… and keep swinging, moving slowly forward, the blade going in big arcs, making a *swack* sound, and with clumps of cut grass flying this way and that. It was hard, hot work, so I took off my T-shirt and hung it from the waistband of my shorts. Grass stuck to my sweaty skin. My back, shoulders, and arms began to ache, but behind me was a lengthening path where I'd swung the scythe, and there was that sweet, hot smell, as the cut grass baked in the sun.

Now and then I had to pause to catch my breath. Through the open windows, I'd hear Hazel's music rolling out in waves. Often she'd be singing along with it, her voice deep and usually in a language I didn't know. But even then I could understand if the music was happy or sad. Twice, she came to the front door, leaning on her cane and holding out a glass of lemonade in her free hand. And once with tears in her eyes.

At first they scared me. *What's wrong?*

"It's so beautiful, that music," she said. "Can you feel it?" She seemed to feel everything. "That's what we're all about."

What in the world did she mean by that? I didn't know how to respond, except to say thanks for the lemonade. It had ice, mint leaves, and real pieces of lemon in it, and because of the lurching way she moved and because her hand shook a little, some of it slurped out over her wrist.

But that didn't bother her. Nor me. What remained in the glass, which was wet, cold, and very sticky, was the best lemonade I've ever tasted.

Looking over the yard, Hazel said, "That's good work, Rusty," though it really wasn't *that good.* I'd cut the grass unevenly, like a bad haircut. But that was another thing that didn't seem to bother her. "Thanks," she said.

And then each time, after I'd finished my lemonade and chewed up the ice, and as Hazel watched from the doorway, I waded into the tall grass again and swung that scythe as hard as I could, hacking through what was in front of me.

• • •

That evening at supper, Lizzy was on the rampage again. "What a stench! You smell like a locker room! And there's bits of straw or something all over you. What have you gotten into now?"

"Nothing," I said, staring at the potato salad that she'd plopped on my plate.

"Why don't you go ahead and tell her?" Dad said. "It's certainly nothing to be ashamed of, Russ. I'd be proud if I was you."

"So tell me," Lizzy said to me in her mean, teasing voice, twirling a loop of hair on her finger.

"That's enough!" Dad said to her, his voice rising. "Rusty got a real summer job. You should be happy for your brother!"

"A job? Rusty? That's a laugh! Doing what?"

"Cutting grass. Raking. Cleaning up!" I blurted out.

"For who?"

"None of your business!"

"Oh, isn't that precious?!" She turned to Dad. "He

doesn't do anything around *here*, except for watering Mom's garden, just standing with the hose, spraying the flowers until they're practically drowned, which isn't work at all! He can't even clean up after *himself!*"

On and on, she went like this, but just then her words didn't hurt so much, because folded tight in my pocket were three crisp five-dollar bills. Though I was right there at our kitchen table, and I could hear Lizzy talking and talking, in my mind I was sitting on the narrow side-deck of my boat. I was on a starboard tack, with the sail full, the sheet (the line that operates the sail) alive in my right hand, the tiller in my left, and my eyes on a thin, silver shaft at the top of my mast. It was sharp and straight as an arrow.

CHAPTER 10
A Gust of Wind

Three days later, after I'd painted the shingles on the south end of Hazel's cottage, I actually bought the wind indicator.

"It's the best one I've got," Buddy D told me at the shop, rubbing his curly red beard. "Doesn't flinch. Looks right into the eye of a gale."

Using a standing ladder I borrowed from Jack, the maintenance man, I clamped the indicator onto the top of my mast, and it worked! When my boat was docked, it showed me the wind's precise direction, even if I couldn't feel a breath of air on my skin. And when I took my boat out on the water that afternoon, it showed me what's called the "apparent wind," a mix of the actual wind and the wind that your boat makes when it's moving, which is the wind that you sail by.

As I'd been doing now for a couple of weeks, I was practicing my tacking. I was learning how to zig-zag upwind, or against the wind. Each time I turned the boat, I was getting better at switching the tiller and sheet from one hand to the other, and moving from one side of the boat to the other—all while ducking beneath the swinging boom, that big horizontal pole attached to the bottom of the sail and to the mast. I'd just finished a pretty smooth tack. I was a quarter mile from the marina. The sky was bright. I was wearing sunglasses. And just as I'd imagined it a few days before, I was sitting on the side-deck, sailing comfortably along in a steady breeze. It was perfect weather. Low waves. I thought I was doing everything right, just like it said in my sailing books.

Then, as I looked up at it, my wind indicator suddenly tilted, and at the same instant the surface of the water nearby turned gray, and a gust of wind from behind me hit the sail with a terrific *WHOOOMPH!!*

Frantically, I held onto the sheet for as long as I could. The tiller jumped from my other hand. And next thing I knew, I was looking up at my sneakers against the sky, and I was flipping backwards over the deck and into the water, while the boat, like a dead fish, rolled over on its side. The sail and mast fell flat on the waves.

Where are my sunglasses? I thought as I coughed and

spat out salty water, my eyes itching, my life jacket pinching under my arms, keeping me afloat. Nothing made sense. *What am I doing here? How did I get here?* The water was freezing and my heart was pounding. Everything was so bright.

In my sailing books, there are instructions for what to do when you capsize. Always stay with your boat. Turn the boat until the hull is facing into the wind. Stand on the keel until you swing the boat upright. Climb in at the stern.

It sounds so easy, just follow directions. But I'm telling you, that's not how it happens, not when one second everything's under control, you're warm and dry, and the next you're shivering and scrambling in the water.

"You okay?!" At first I thought it was a voice in my head. A moment later, Jack, along with another guy in a bathing suit, appeared nearby in his motorboat. "Hey Sonny, you need a hand?" he yelled over the noise of his idling motor. Jack called everyone under sixty "Sonny," even if he knew you.

"I'm all right," I called back, though I was afraid I might cry. I was treading water now, staying close to my boat, but I was still spitting and shivering. With both arms, I grabbed and held onto the keel that stuck out of the hull horizontally, about a foot above the water.

"Why don't you come aboard?" Jack said. "Lenny here can take care of your boat, get it upright and sail it back."

Something about this made me clench inside. "No," I said. "I can do it."

"You think so?"

"Yes!"

The two men looked at each other. "Well, we're not going anywhere. I'll give you a couple shots at it, and then I'm hauling you out of the water with my bare hands, if I have to. I don't want you going blue on me, Sonny!"

Climbing onto the keel of a sailboat floating on its side is like pulling yourself straight out of a swimming pool and onto a low diving board, except that everything's swaying and slippery. I got my chest up on the keel once and slid off. Another time, I got my feet on it, squatting, and fell off again.

"Give me another chance!" I yelled. And now I *was* crying. On the third try, I managed to stand on the keel while clutching the side-deck, but I wasn't heavy enough to push the keel beneath the water and turn the boat right side up.

"Hold on!" the man named Lenny said, and he dove in and swam right up to me. "You just need a little more meat on your bones!"

He was as big as a walrus, with lots of meat on *his* bones, and when he pulled down on the keel, the hull slowly turned upright, the mast and sail rising off the water, as I scrambled up and over the side and back into my boat.

"Good!" Jack yelled from the motorboat, as Lenny

swam back toward him.

Water streamed off me. The boat rocked. My heart kept pounding. Luckily, there were no more gusts just then, so as Jack and Lenny watched, I was able to grab the sheet and the tiller. Jack gave me the thumbs up sign. I sat again on the starboard deck and checked my wind indicator that was still clamped to the top of the mast. Water sloshed around my shins, bogging down the boat. Still, I managed to turn and sail slowly back toward the marina, as the motorboat followed behind.

Drifting into the dock where I always tie up, I saw Hazel waiting in her wheelchair, with her binoculars on a shoe lace around her neck. "You all right?"

"Yeah."

"What happened?"

What does it look like? I said to myself. "I capsized."

"Well, as long as you're okay… It happens to everyone who calls himself a sailor. How did it happen?"

"I don't know. A big gust came out of nowhere, and the boat turned over."

"And did you turn over away from or toward the wind?"

By then I was out of the boat, my sneakers *squeech, squeech, squeeching* with every step. I tied the bow and stern lines to cleats on the dock. "Away from it," I said. "Why are you asking me all this?" I was embarrassed enough already.

"Hmmm," Hazel said. "When the gust came, did you let go of the sheet?"

"No. I held on as long as I could."

"All right. Let me give you a tip. Sometimes you're right to hold onto the sheet for all you're worth. But sometimes you get hit so hard that it's best to let go and let the wind have its way. You'll get the knack of it. Don't worry."

Well, I did worry. How would I ever know these things? Would I capsize again? I wasn't even sure if I wanted to learn to sail anymore.

I got back into the boat and started bailing. We didn't speak until Hazel said in a lighter tone, "By the way, I see you have something new on your boat!" She seemed to notice every detail when it came to boats. "It's a beauty!" As if on cue, the wind indicator swung to follow a slight change in the breeze. She smiled and gave me a wink that said we shared a secret. "Where'd you ever get the money for that?"

CHAPTER 11

A Rainstorm

The next week, the third week in July, it rained on and off a lot. The hull of my boat filled again with water, and I didn't get out sailing. In summer school, we started on measurement—inches, feet, yards, meters, and miles.

"How about *nautical miles?*" Hazel said one afternoon when I was doing homework in her kitchen. "Anything about that in your math book?"

"No."

"Well, that's crazy! Nautical miles beat regular miles every time. A nautical mile is longer. So tell me this. If a knot is one nautical mile per hour—which it is—and say you're sailing your boat at ten knots while somebody racing you on land is driving at ten regular, boring miles per hour, who's going faster? Who's going to win?"

"That's easy. I am."

"Right! You ought to tell your teacher about that. Whoever wrote your math book wasn't a sailor!"

• • •

At supper a couple days later, Dad told Lizzy and me that he'd talked to Mom's doctors and they'd said she was "stabilizing," but they couldn't say much more than that. I didn't know how to feel about this. It didn't seem bad, and it didn't seem good. Mostly it just felt like more of the same, more waiting.

In the six weeks since Mom had left, I hadn't completely gotten used to her not being home. I'd written those three letters—all in my best handwriting—that she still hadn't answered. I'd told her that I had a sailboat that I was learning to sail. I'd asked her if she was in a nice room, if maybe there were flowers there. I'd asked her if she'd made any friends and if she had any of her favorite books with her—I would send some if she wanted them. In all my letters, I wrote at the end,

When are you coming home? Soon I hope.

Love, Rusty

At night, especially as I was turning off my lamp, I still listened for her steps on the stairs before she'd come into my room to talk and to say "Sleep tight." Some mornings, I still waited for her to open my curtains and say in her coaxing voice, "Another school day. Rise and shine." Though I didn't feel as bad as I did those first nights, there were lots of times when I couldn't fall asleep and I couldn't stop thinking, *Will she **ever** come home?* One night the shapes in my room seemed to move—my belt slithering across the rug, the knob on my closet door turning with a click—and I had to reach over and turn on my lamp to make everything still. Then I read my sailing books again.

At other times, it didn't surprise me that I couldn't hear Mom's steps on the stairs, or that my curtains were closed when I woke up, or that her chair was empty at the kitchen table, or that she wasn't around to make tea for herself and a sandwich for me when I came home from summer school. This was just the way things were. When I wasn't at Hazel's, I drifted through those rainy afternoons, killing time in the work shed, or watching TV in a sleepy fog. I didn't know what was worse, getting numb like that and not feeling all I was missing. Or feeling it all—which really hurt.

Meanwhile, as the days passed, Dad seemed to have a harder and harder time, though he tried not to show it. Things kept slipping his mind—and not just things like forgetting to do the wash. One night he put a carton of ice cream away in the cupboard and bananas in the freezer. And one Thursday, his day off, while Lizzy was at camp and I was at school, he didn't close the upstairs windows around the house when a big storm came through. If Mom was home and her normal self, she'd have run around to every room "to batten down the hatches." But somehow Dad forgot the windows that day. So when I arrived at lunchtime, took off my raincoat, and went up to my room, the curtains were soaked, and my sailing books, open on the windowsill, looked like heads of lettuce. The pages were drenched, wrinkled, and curled, with some of the pictures so smeared that I couldn't tell what they were about.

"Oh, no!" Dad said, when he came up about ten minutes later and saw me sitting at my desk with two boxes of Kleenex, trying to dry and flatten the pages. He looked horrified. "Russ, I'm so sorry. How could I have forgotten?"

Many of the pages were stuck together. There were whole chapters I couldn't read now, some of them my favorites: "Sailing Downwind," "Reading Wind on the Water," and "Leaving from and Returning to a

Mooring." Though I tried, I couldn't say a word.

Dad grabbed the chair from the hall, sat beside me, and pulled me close, where I felt his long, deep, shaky breaths, and he could probably feel mine.

At last, when I could speak, I said, "I can get some other books." Then I said, "It's okay. It's going to be all right," which was something *he* often told *me*. A moment later, I added, "It's no big deal."

Though both of us knew that it was.

CHAPTER 12

The Painting

On those rainy afternoons when I was at Hazel's cottage, she had me do inside jobs—after we'd had lunch and I'd done some math, of course. One day, in her bedroom, I cleared out everything in a closet that stank of mothballs: shirts, heavy coats, and creased pants on wooden hangers, neckties on a little ladder-like thing, and on a shelf, a straw hat like Huck Finn might wear. These were Hazel's husband's old clothes, and it felt creepy to hold them in my arms and fold them into the big plastic bags for the Next-to-New sale at the Congregational Church.

"Time to pass these things along," Hazel said with a sigh. "If you see anything you or your dad can use, you're welcome to it. Except for the straw hat. That stays."

I said no thanks, and as I tied up the plastic bags, she told me how, after she and her husband,

Malcolm, got married, they moved near the city on the mainland. In her eyes, she had a watery look that made me feel strange, like maybe I shouldn't have been there. "For thirty years that's where we lived. We raised the kids. But when they moved away, we moved here, right where I grew up. Funny how you come back to things."

Later that afternoon, she asked me to wash the insides of the windows in the room down the hall where she'd disappeared on that first day I'd visited. I'd never been in there. The door was usually closed. It turned out to be her studio, which, though it wasn't big, felt bright and airy, even on a rainy day. It was entirely different than the rest of the cottage—at some point it must have been renovated. The ceiling, with a skylight in it, opened up to the rafters. There were big windows on two sides, and near the largest window stood a tall easel on three legs. On either side were a couple of beat-up tables crammed with curled-up paint tubes, sketch pads, erasers, rags, cans, bowls, and jars filled with brushes and pencils. Drips, smudges, and speckles of color covered everything. Unframed paintings of birds and beaches leaned against all the walls. The little room reminded me of our work shed at home, with our tools scattered over the bench, the smells of epoxy and cedar shavings, and sawdust everywhere, when I'd been repairing my boat.

The room—and not just its light—seemed to brighten Hazel's face, and it made me feel better too, like all the rainy days didn't matter. "This is where I work," she said, opening her arms wide. "This is me! I love it here!"

"And these are the things you sell at the Art Barn?"

"Yes, but I don't sell all of them. Most are like post cards, just cheap souvenirs: the pictures of gulls on pilings and kids building sand castles. I can do those well enough, the ones that tourists take home to prove they've been on vacation. But now and then I paint one that's a keeper, one that I can't let go. Like this one here. It's almost finished." She seemed suddenly proud and bashful all at once, like a girl who beats all the boys in a race. "It started with a sketch—things always start with a sketch—and grew from there. I've been working on it a couple days."

We went closer to the easel. On its ledge stood a small painting of the ocean, about a foot across by nine inches high, that was different from the others. For one thing, you could really see how her brush had put on the paint, sometimes in curls, dabs, or skittery lines. For another, you could see how the colors were all mixed up, how the blue of the water had threads, blobs, and smudges of gray, green, black, and brown. And here's the last thing: looking at it, you almost lost your balance. Everything seemed cockeyed, like the painting was hanging at some crazy angle. It made you tilt your head, because the horizon of huge, choppy waves slanted wildly to the left. Closer, the waves were white on top, and spray streamed back over them. Closer yet, the edge of a sail ballooned with wind. And in the front, right at the bottom, I noticed the inside curve of a boat's side-deck. It, too, was at a crazy angle to the horizon.

Still looking with my head tilted, I swore that I was right inside that boat. Or I mean I was barely inside it, leaning way out over the waves, every muscle stretched to breaking, holding on for dear life, trying to keep the boat from heeling (tilting) too far, as it shot across the canvas, faster than I'd ever sailed.

"That's amazing!" was all I could say for a moment. Then I asked, "How do you know what it's like to sail like that?"

"Long story," she said. "It goes way back. But I'll keep it short." She stared at a spot above my head where there wasn't anything to see. "In the winters, my father worked in Cantwell's boatyard here. During summers, he sailed tourists all around the bay and the sound in a rented sloop-rigged cruiser. He could sail in pitch dark, in any weather, in any wind. He knew every rock and shoal. When I was your age, he took me along and showed me the ropes—literally. Often we sailed alone, just him and me. Usually I'd crew for him, but now and then he let me take the helm. He let me tack and jibe. Sometimes we'd run wing-and-wing. It was scary, but I did it. Those were the greatest days..."

Her voice trailed off, and she brushed a frizzy strand of hair from her forehead. How long had it been since she was a kid? How long since she'd sailed like that?

Her eyes came back from wherever they'd been. "I'm glad you like the painting," she said.

CHAPTER 13

Dear Rusty

On one of those sleepy, early afternoons between rainy days, when Hazel was at the Art Barn and I came straight home from summer school, I brought in the mail from the basket beside our front door. There were the usual advertising flyers and some bills that would make Dad say "Ugh." And then I saw two envelopes, one addressed to Lizzy and the other to me, in Mom's neat handwriting. My heart jumped. What would she say? Could she be coming back soon?

Lizzy and Dad wouldn't be home for hours, but I took my letter right up to my room, closed the door, and tore open the envelope. The letter was two whole pages! I'd never gotten one so long.

July 26

Dear Rusty,
Thank you for your letters, which I keep in my pocket or here on my desk where I can hold them and see them and think of you, as if you're as close to me right now as your letters are in my hands.

How are you doing? How is summer school? How are things at home? I know it's rough, and I wish I was with you. Please try not to be too sad. Keep doing what makes you happy. You wrote that Mr. Clark gave you his boat and that you've repaired it and are sailing it. That's wonderful! I'm so proud of you. How big is the boat? Does it have a name? I can't wait to see it.

You asked me what my days are like. On my good days, I eat in the dining hall with all the other women—there are only women here. I have lots of doctors and a counselor who's a sort of teacher and coach. With her, I have meetings, or we walk in the woods, and often I go to workshops, group sessions, and exercise classes. On my not-so-good days, someone comes and helps me get going in the morning, and I spend most of those days with the horses, which my counselor says is a good idea. Sometimes I brush them. Sometimes I feed them. The horses are so big and calm, their eyes so steady, and somehow they seem to know and trust me without my having to say anything. My favorite is a gray horse named Zephyr, which means a gentle breeze.

I've never written a letter like this and the one I just wrote to Lizzy. I've tried to write you a half dozen times, but I couldn't do it, I didn't know how, because I knew I should try to explain what's happened and why I'm here, even if I can't understand it myself. The doctors say I've been very depressed, though for the life of me, I can't find a reason for it. Your dad is a wonderful husband, and you and Lizzy are wonderful kids. I couldn't ask for more. Still, there are times when everything seems to get dark and sad, when I think I'm not a good mother, not a good wife, not a good anything, and I get so frightened, and I feel like I'm swirling down and down, everything narrowing and draining, like into a funnel. Do you mind me telling you all this? I know it's hard to understand. I'm not as strong as I'd like to be. Inside me are cracks, Rusty, like the ones you described in your boat, and like you, I'm trying to mend them.

In all your letters you asked when I'll come home. Believe me, I wish I could come this minute. I miss my garden. And mostly I miss you, Lizzy, and Dad so much, right here in my bones. There are nights when I think I might run away and find my way back. But what am I thinking? Me? Run away? I hope I can come home soon. But right now I just don't know.

I love you with all my heart.
Mom

I read the letter again and again, my heart jumping and sinking each time. What did she mean by her "not-so-good days?" How bad were they? Were they worse than her bad days at home? Was she getting better or not? How long would they keep her there?

I thought I might write a letter straight back to her, but I felt too confused to do it right then. I folded Mom's letter and put it in my pocket. Then I went downstairs and outside, and biked over to the dock. I stepped into my boat, but didn't feel like sailing. I had no idea where I'd go. From my toolbox in the compartment under the stern seat, I got a rag and Brasso and started polishing all the hardware—the cleats, the chocks, the bow handle, even the little grommets on the sail.

I must have polished that hardware like crazy, because I didn't even notice Jack when he walked past and probably said hello. I only noticed him when he'd come back, stopped, and stared at me. "You okay?"

Startled, I said, "Yes, I'm okay."

And eventually I was. It felt good to rub away the salt and grit and leave the hardware gleaming. A breeze rocked the boat and made the rubber fenders *squinch.* The sun warmed my back, things seemed to slow down and relax, and in my head I wrote a letter to Mom that I'd actually write when I went home. I'd say thanks for telling me about the horses, and that I was glad she liked them and they liked her. I'd say that math was okay, though it was hard to tell because everything depended on a few tests later in the summer. I'd let her know that my boat was a catboat, with the mast way up near the bow. I'd say that it didn't have a name yet, and that it was a small boat, and broad beamed, its width about half its length. I wouldn't tell her that once I'd capsized. I wouldn't tell her that Dad, Lizzy, and I were having a hard time, that Dad kept forgetting things, and Lizzy always seemed mad, and when I was home, I just wanted to stay in my room, and some nights I couldn't sleep. I also wouldn't mention that I was working for Hazel—somehow that seemed too complicated. Finally I *would* tell her that I was sorry she couldn't come home yet, and that I hoped it'd be soon. I'd sign my name after I wrote *Love.* Then under that, I'd add a P.S.:

I have your letter in my pocket too.

• • •

That evening at supper, Lizzy barely said a word, so I knew that she'd read her own letter before Dad had come home, and now, like me, she was thinking about it.

"Both of you are downright courteous tonight. What's wrong?" Dad said, passing the hamburgers.

I didn't feel like saying anything about my letter in front of Lizzy, and she didn't feel like saying anything in front of me. We ate, then washed and dried the dishes in silence, and Dad just let us be.

A couple hours later, when I was in bed, trying

to keep my mind on my new sailing books from the library, Dad came in and sat on the edge of my bed. He ran his hand through his hair. "Did you happen to get a letter from Mom? Is that why you and Lizzy are so quiet?"

I didn't say anything, but I guess he could see the answer in my face.

He nodded that he understood. "Not exactly the sort of news you were hoping for, I suppose?"

"No, not exactly."

"Should I turn off your lamp?"

"Okay."

He turned it off, but didn't stand up, which meant he still wanted to talk. "We're going to get through this, Russ. You know that, right? We're all going to be okay," he said, though I couldn't see his eyes to make sure that he really believed it.

For a few minutes more, he sat there, both of us quiet, as if our ears were almost like hands, reaching out and feeling for something in the dark.

Eventually, he patted my arm, got up, and went out of my bedroom. I heard him knock on Lizzy's door on the other side of the hall, then open and shut it behind him. I imagine they had a conversation a lot like the one I'd just had, as Dad now sat on the edge of *her* bed. I could hear their low voices, but not their exact words, and I could almost feel them thinking in the long pauses between their words. Fifteen minutes later, Dad came out, went downstairs, and closed up the house for the night. Then I heard Lizzy, my proud, pain-in-the-neck, hard-as-nails sister, sobbing and sobbing in her dark bedroom, though not very loud, because she must have had her face in her pillow.

CHAPTER 14

Whispering Pines?

When I went to Hazel's cottage two days later on another rainy afternoon, I found the front door closed and a folded note thumbtacked to it. On the outside in careful printing the note said, "Rusty." Here's what I read inside:

> Let yourself in. You know where the key is. Sorry I'm not here. I forgot to tell you that I have an appointment this afternoon. Marigold has eaten. I should be back by 4:00. If I'm late, your pay is on the kitchen counter. Lock up and replace the key when you leave. Why don't you finish cleaning and dusting the bookcases in the living room? That should keep you busy! H.

I slid the key from beneath the gull-shaped mailbox and let myself in. How strange to be alone in a house that isn't yours—or almost alone, because, as soon as I'd opened the door, Marigold greeted me, sliding against my shins. I rubbed her back and hung my raincoat on a peg beside Hazel's cane. When I walked into the living room between the stacks of magazines, I could hear the floorboards creaking, and from everywhere came the sounds of rain, a drumming on the roof, a waterfall splashing over the clogged-up gutters, and a steady *plink-plink-plinking* in a pot on the floor beneath a leak in the ceiling.

In the kitchen, Marigold's bowls were almost full. And there, as usual, were some carrot sticks, a sandwich, my napkin in its shackle ring, and a glass of water on the table beside a note that said, "Ice cream in the fridge." Three five-dollar bills were fanned on the counter beside the sink… Then it struck me. Why couldn't I just take that money and leave *without* spending the afternoon choking on years of dust? What was to stop me from taking any other money that might be in drawers or in the little wooden boxes on Hazel's bureau?

The truth was, nothing would stop me, nothing at all—except everything that I was feeling because she trusted me like that.

I ate my lunch, washed the dishes and, with Marigold curled on my lap, did exactly twenty minutes of math, converting inches into millimeters, and meters into yards and feet. Then I got started in the living room. I vacuumed everything, dusted, then polished the bookcases with lemon oil, until every shelf shined and I could see the grain of the wood.

When I went back into the kitchen to fix myself some ice cream, I noticed a brochure on the counter beside the refrigerator: "Whispering Pines: A Senior Living Home." On the front was a picture of some happy old people, a few in wheelchairs, doing arm exercises on a beautiful green lawn. Inside were more pictures: a gray-haired couple talking with a smiling doctor wearing a white coat and a stethoscope, and other people playing cards and laughing around a square table. There were sections called "Maintenance-Free Living," "Private Rooms," and "Compassionate and Dignified Care," which were circled in black ink. I didn't recognize the address of the place, but it must have been on the mainland, because it was "right near the heart of the metro area." "Come join us," the brochure said, "and enjoy your golden years!"

Whispering Pines? A shiver went through me, and I just stared at the brochure. Was it true? Was Hazel thinking of moving and living somewhere else? In some special "home"?

I was carefully putting the things back on the bookshelves, when I heard Hazel at the door. "Good, you're still here," she said, rolling in. She unclamped the umbrella from the handle of her wheelchair and put it aside. She looked at the shining bookcases. "Nice!" Then joint by joint, she raised herself up and stood with her cane, but glancing at me, she stopped. "What's wrong? Some news about your mom?"

How could she know these things? I thought of telling her about Mom's letter, but there really wasn't any news. "No," I said.

"Well, something's bugging you. It's all over your face." Despite her cane and tottering legs, she could stand like a fence post in front of you. "Tell me," she said. And the funny thing was, something seemed to be bugging her, too.

"It's nothing," I said.

"Baloney! I'm not moving until you tell me. You've got to be the worst liar in the world!"

"All right," I said after a moment. I could tell her at least part of what was bugging me: "That brochure beside your refrigerator. What's it all about?"

Briefly, she seemed taken off guard. Then she waved her free hand, as if to wave the brochure away. "Oh that. It's not important."

For a few seconds we were quiet, and I was about to say *Baloney!* myself, but before I could, she said in a different tone, "All right, Rusty. I'll level with you. That brochure is Charlie and Ann's doing. My son and daughter—one of them sent it. Such worrywarts. Because they're hardly ever here, their imaginations get the best of them. They're afraid I'll get sick. They say I'm too old to be alone and take care of myself. They want to move me to someplace 'safe' and 'more appropriate,' they call it, some so-called 'home,' with nobody but nurses, cranky old geezers like me, and televisions going at a million decibels every waking hour of the day. Does that sound like a *home* to you? Or a *life?!*" Hazel's voice was getting louder. I'd never heard her so angry. She shook her head in disgust. "No way I'm going to a place like that! Not while I'm still breathing! You can take my word for it!"

Then she stopped, looked at me, and smiled. She shook her head again, but this time like she was impatient and disgusted with herself. "Listen to me, ranting like this. End of speech. End of temper tantrum. Now let's have a good look at these beautiful bookcases!"

CHAPTER 15
A Present

During the first week of August, we started a long stretch of good weather, and on most afternoons I got out to practice sailing again. That was also when I got a postcard from Walter—no phones were allowed at his camp. He wrote that all the kids there had head lice and had to wash their hair with something gross, thick, and smelly. I think he was homesick, and I wrote him, saying I'd be around when he got back. I told him about some things I was doing: how in my boat I was trying to teach myself to jibe, a tricky maneuver that lets you turn through the wind when it's behind you, but I hadn't nailed it yet. Neither of us mentioned the argument we'd had before he'd left. I didn't tell him that I'd capsized, and I sure didn't say anything about Hazel.

Then in the second week of August, I got another, shorter letter from Mom. It said that she "might be getting better," though she still didn't know when she could come home, which was also what Dad said after calling her that week.

Meanwhile, on Hazel's afternoons off, I kept working at her cottage, raking in all that money, which I put in a sock in my bureau. Except for another day when she had another appointment—a "follow-up," she called it—I ate lunch with her and did math as she worked in her studio. Next I'd tackle whatever job she told me to do, but more and more she let me do whatever jobs I wanted. I had the feeling that she cared less about *what* I did than that I earned my money by working hard at *something*. One day, I brushed a fresh coat of blue paint, the color of the sky, on her front door. On another, I climbed up a ladder I found behind the cottage and cleaned all the old leaves out of the gutters. Extending the ladder, I got up on the roof and fixed the leak with some tarry stuff that Dad had brought home from the hardware store. When it rained on the following day, Hazel and I celebrated. Water rushed through her clean gutters and downspouts. Not a drop *plinked* in the pot on the living room floor! So I took the pot back to the kitchen, Hazel washed it, and we used it to make vanilla pudding. "Beats rainwater any day!" she said, as she spooned the pudding into bowls.

Around then, we began taking our mid-afternoon "coffee break," we called it, though neither of us drank coffee. We'd both stop what we were doing and come into the living room for ten or fifteen minutes, each of us with a glass of lemonade. Hazel would sit in her armchair with the newspaper or a book, and Marigold and I would lie on the floor. During those breaks, I liked to fool around with that brass compass from one of Hazel's shelves. She said it used to be her dad's. I'd flip open the lid and hold it across the palm of my hand—it felt like it belonged there. Leveling and turning it until the red arrow pointed at N, I felt that I knew more about where I was and where things were around me. I could see, for example, if Marigold was north, east, south, or west of me, and, counting the little hatch marks around the rim, I could tell by how many degrees. Often I'd look through the *National Geographic* and *Nature* magazines, and if I thought it might qualify as "fascinating," I'd show Hazel what I was reading. Or once, out of the blue, she asked me, "What's a three letter word that means 'fiend'?" She always said that doing the crosswords kept her brain from "getting moldy."

"Liz," I couldn't help answering. "L. I. Z. Short for Lizzy. That ought to work for fiend."

Over her glasses, Hazel gave me a look. "Imp," she said, writing it out. "I. M. P. I think that will work better."

In fact, since she'd gotten her first letter from Mom, Lizzy was becoming less and less of a fiend. At the supper table, she seemed to smolder, but didn't go nuts and rip into me. Maybe she didn't care as much, or maybe she didn't have the heart for it anymore. Or maybe her new attitude had a little to do with my math. At summer school, we'd started on geometry—rectangles, trapezoids, triangles, figuring out perimeters and areas—which, because I could actually *see* that stuff, I could understand it. Once, for instance, Hazel said she was just dying to know the area of my sail, and after I'd measured its base and height, which I multiplied and then divided by two, I got it: exactly 146 square feet. While I wasn't getting Lizzy-style grades, I'd been finishing my homework, doing better, and so I was a smaller target for Lizzy to fire at, if she felt like firing at all. When at breakfast one day I told her and Dad that I got a B on a big test, she just sat there, dazed, like all the air had gone out of her.

"Terrific!" Dad said. "That means you'll probably pass, right?"

"I hope so," I said.

And when I told Hazel about it on a warm afternoon two days later, I don't think I'd ever seen her so happy. "Let's take today off!" she said. "With pay!" And though we didn't spit watermelon seeds that afternoon, we did some fun and goofy things. In the kitchen, we played slapjack, whamming the table when one of us turned over a jack, so that Hazel's pills in their plastic containers leaped up like jumping beans. Though I eventually won the game and got the whole deck, Hazel didn't give up without a fight. Her hands, like crabs, were sneaky fast.

Then I thought of another way to use a few of the playing cards—something Walter and I used to do with our bikes—and Hazel said okay, she had an extra deck, and the cards were worn out anyway. In the front yard again, I attached two cards, each with a clothespin, to the cross pieces on either side of her wheelchair, so the cards stuck between the spokes. When she wheeled down the path, with me jogging behind and the cards fluttering and smacking in the spokes, her wheelchair sounded like a motorcycle. She sped up, going as fast as she could.

"I should wear a helmet and a black leather jacket!" she said, breathing hard, when we returned.

"Can I try it?" Another of those questions that just popped out of me.

"Sure!"

I fetched her cane for her. She got out of her wheelchair and stood in the shade, and I got in. I'd never been in a wheelchair before. It makes you feel small and clumsy. I couldn't even keep myself going straight. My sweaty hands slipped on the rims, and the little front wheels wiggled every which way.

"Hard on your port wheel!" Hazel called. "Ease off on the starboard, or you'll capsize!"

When I came back, panting and my arms feeling like mush, she was smiling to herself, leaning back against the trunk of the tree, and dabbing her forehead with a Kleenex.

"This is harder than sailing," I said. "You know, they make wheelchairs with batteries and motors so you don't have to wear yourself out."

She looked at me, frowning. "And they also make motors for boats, so you don't have to sail." She made a huffing sound that meant she'd never heard of anything so ridiculous. "Why would I want a motor to push me when I've got two good hands and arms?!"

Later, drinking Coke floats, another special treat, we sat out on her patio in the warm, slanting sun.

In that light, Hazel's wrinkles seemed deep enough to slide coins into, and I could see small hollows at her temples. Her skin just then looked thin, like you could almost see right *into* her, while her happiness seemed to shine right out, and I could feel it too.

"I'm proud of you, Rusty."

"It was only a B," I said. "It might have been an easy test."

"No, I'm not just talking about your test. The math is just part of it. There's all the work you've done here this summer. There's the fun we've had. There's the sailing you've taught yourself. And goodness knows what else you've managed to do, while..." She trailed off, meaning but not saying, *you've been without your mom*.

I didn't know how to reply to this, so I shut up. I could tell Hazel had more to say: "Whether you know it or not, you're onto something. You've kept your head up. You've done what you had to do—the math, I mean. And you've thrown all you had at what you love—the sailing."

I wanted to tell her that she'd helped me out, but she went right on. "That's great stuff. And here's the trick: to keep doing what you love as long as you can. Even if it gets difficult. Or *because* it's difficult. I'm trying to remember that too."

With our straws, we sucked our floats down to the gurgly bottom, and Hazel set her glass on the side table. She seemed to be thinking, and then she said, "I've wanted to give you something, and maybe this is the time. Stay here." She got herself up and hobbled inside. A couple minutes later, she returned with something about the size of my math textbook wrapped in yellow paper and a white bow.

"For you," she said, and gave it to me with her free hand. She sat down again in her chair.

"A math book!" I said. "Just what I wanted!"

She laughed. "Go ahead and open it."

I did.

And like the first time I saw it, it took my breath away. It was that painting that had been on her easel, now finished and framed with varnished cedar, the same wood that my boat is made of. I held the painting across my knees, looking at it, and it seemed like the most wonderful and exciting thing in the world: that heeling boat slicing through heaving water. And again I could swear I was sailing it, everything rushing and slanted. I could feel the wind and spray.

"But this is *your* painting," I said. "You said it was 'a keeper,' one that you couldn't let go."

"I know. It *is* special." Her voice was as serious as I'd ever heard it. "That's why I want you to have it and keep it. It means more to me if it's in *your* hands. It can't stay in mine forever."

At that moment, I couldn't help but look at her hands, with their bony fingers and tunneling veins, as they lay on her lap with that little tremor, shivering like tuning forks.

And then I realized that one of those hands had held a brush and stroked or dabbed paint onto that canvas. So the tremor in her hands was *in* that painting, in those dancing, choppy waves, in the skittering spray, in that tilting horizon, in everything I was looking at that seemed so alive and wild.

"Are you sure you want me to have it?"

"I'm positive." Her eyes never left my face.

"Okay." I said. "I'll take good care of it."

"I know you will," she said.

CHAPTER 16

Guess What

Hazel paid me, then told me to go on home a half hour early that day. I deserved it, she said, and besides, the heat and all the excitement were making her tired. She needed a rest. I wrapped the painting up in the yellow paper and then for good measure in layers of newspaper, before putting it into my backpack. At home, I slid it into the bottom drawer of my bureau with my folded winter shirts and my money sock, where I knew it'd be safe while I figured out what to do with it. Then on the next day, I came straight home from summer school, took the painting out to the work shed, turned it over on a towel on the bench, and carefully drilled two small, shallow holes, each on either side of the back of the frame. Into each hole I twisted a screw eye and fastened a strong wire between them. In my room, I drilled a hole into the wall above my pillow, then hammered in a nail, and that's where I hung Hazel's painting.

"Where did that come from?" Dad asked that evening, the first time he saw it.

"From Hazel. You know, the lady I work for. She painted it. You can see her initial, H., right there in the corner."

"How much did you pay for it?"

"Nothing. She gave it to me."

And whether it was that particular price or the painting itself, or both, Dad seemed to approve. "She's a piece of work, that lady. But she's got a knack." He bent close to the picture and studied it. "Look at those waves!" Then he tilted his head to get his bearings.

Just then, his phone rang, and he went into his bedroom to answer it, closing the door behind him. He spoke for a couple of minutes, and I could only hear him in snippets. In a strange, excited voice, he said, "Yes… Of course… When?" and "I'll be there."

When he came back in my room, he had tears in his eyes, but he didn't look sad. For a second, he just stood there, stunned, like he didn't know what to do with himself, his big hands hanging down.

He called for Lizzy to quickly come in.

"What is it?" she said, standing in her pajamas in the doorway.

"Guess what," Dad said.

"What?" we said.

"Mom's coming home." He said this as if he couldn't believe it, though he wanted to with all his heart. "I'm picking her up. On Friday. In just three days."

I don't think any of us slept that night. We were all too excited. I saw Lizzy's light go on a few times, that slot of yellow beneath her door. I heard Dad get up at least twice, once to open the medicine cabinet in the bathroom and probably take his aspirin, and another time to go downstairs and probably make himself a snack. From my bed, I watched the moonlight climb and fall, inch by inch, over the clumps of clothes and shoes on my rug. Through my window, I heard nuts and twigs falling from the trees, and the waves that kept lapping and lapping.

We were all up early the next morning, and Lizzy was her old camp director self again. She called into my room, "Get up!" Her eyes were on fire. "Lots to do today and tomorrow!" Before I went to school and after she'd already vacuumed the hall, she told me to clean up my room: "If you can clean up for your old lady girlfriend, then you can sure do it here!"

"Get lost!" I said. "I can do what I want!" But to tell the truth, I didn't mind cleaning up. I didn't want Mom tripping over my clothes and backpack, or seeing the big balls of dust beneath my bed, or my desk like a bomb had hit it.

When I came home from school that afternoon—it wasn't a day that I worked at Hazel's—Dad was already there. Somehow, he'd arranged to get out of work early, and he was spraying and scrubbing the windows in the kitchen, while the dryer hummed and the washing machine chugged in the basement. The whole house smelled of bleach, Windex, detergent, and Lemon Pledge. The sink was scoured. The kitchen floor gleamed. And Lizzy wasn't even home from camp yet!

After he'd finished with the windows, Dad took me with him to Mickey's, where we both got haircuts. "Try to sit still," Mickey said to me as he snipped around my ears. And while he waited his turn in the big chair, Dad couldn't keep his own foot from twitching. "You guys must have hot dates!" Mickey said, giving me a nudge with his elbow and shaking hair from the sheet that had been around my neck. "I wonder who are the lucky ladies." I saw Dad's face get red. Later, when he'd walked us to the door, Mickey waved goodbye and wished us well: "You both look like a million bucks. Smooth sailing!"

CHAPTER 17

Casting Off

The next day I went to Hazel's to work as usual, and I told her right away—or almost right away. Sitting down and pulling our napkins out of their rings, she looked at me and said, "What's up? If you were a girl, I'd say you have a bee in your bonnet. Something's buzzing around inside you. And you got a haircut, too. It's handsome."

"I have some news," I said. Then it was hard to say.

"Yes?" she said, though I had the feeling she may have sensed it already. "Cat got your tongue? What is it?"

"My mom."

"Yes?"

"She's coming home."

"Wonderful! When?"

"Tomorrow. Dad's leaving to get her on the first ferry in the morning. He's already filled up the car with gas. He'll bring her home in time for supper!" And then the rest of it spilled out in a rush: how we were cleaning everything in sight; how Lizzy had baked cupcakes; how I'd cut the grass; how I'd already put a tea bag in Mom's favorite cup; and how Dad, on his way home from work that evening, would buy some special flowers.

As I said all this, Marigold jumped up into Hazel's lap, and Hazel listened patiently and thoughtfully, not meeting my eyes or eating her sandwich, but looking down at Marigold. "That will make a nice homecoming for your mom," she said, though I don't think that was most on her mind.

We started eating our sandwiches, but didn't talk for a few minutes. Then Hazel turned to look at me again. Her voice was calm and cautious: "Do you remember that first day on the dock, when you were bailing out your boat and I was being pushy, to say the least?"

"Yes."

"And do you remember what you said, that you might take me sailing 'sometime'?"

"Yes."

She paused for a second and went on, not being pushy at all: "Well, what would you think about taking that trip now?"

"This afternoon?"

"The best things, you know, are often unplanned. Let's do it. Why not?"

"What if we tip over?"

"We won't. You're a better sailor now. And if we capsize, we'll both have on life jackets. Someone will help us."

This still sounded risky. "Why don't we wait? How about in a couple of months when I'll be even better?"

Again Hazel paused. Then she said something that puzzled me: "I think it might be now or never." She looked away and let Marigold rub her back against her palm.

"What do you mean?"

She didn't answer.

"So you're asking me to take another day off?"

"What's another day off in the long run of things, especially if it's a great day for sailing? And of course I'll pay you as usual."

At the moment, this was hard to argue with, and I was still puzzling over what she'd meant by "now or never." Did she think I might stop sailing sometime soon, that I might lose my interest in it? Or that she, for some reason, might lose *her* interest? "All right," I finally said. I had no idea if we could get her into my boat, to say nothing of actually sailing with her aboard. "I doubt we can do it, but I guess we can try."

So that's what we did, and without even finishing our sandwiches. Hazel grabbed a green windbreaker from a hook by the door, got in her wheelchair, and with a little extra energy in her arms, we went straight out, down her walk, out Oak Lane, around the wall on Bayshore Street, and down to the dock, where her wheels *thunk-thunked* across the planks. Those 2×6 boards were still stacked near the end, and Hazel asked me to set two of them parallel to one another, a few feet apart, to make a ramp down into my boat, which was tied in its usual spot.

"Are you sure you don't want to try to get in using your cane?" I asked. "I could help you." What if, in her wheelchair, she tumbled off the boards?

"It's too big a step down," Hazel said. "But I can handle this." Luckily, the water in the marina was calm. I tightened the bow and stern lines, so the boat was snug to the dock. "Wedge those boards in so they don't move," she said, lining up her wheels with them.

With a grunt, she tipped her front wheels over the ends of the boards. Soon her back wheels followed, as the boat dipped slightly and the fenders made their *squinching* sounds. For an instant, I thought she might veer off the boards, which had only a few inches to spare on either side of her wheels. But the boat held steady, and she held herself steady, concentrating, her arms locked and her gnarled fingers gripping the wheel rims with all her might. Then letting the rims slide slowly through her hands, she rolled down the ramp, straight as a string, until she was aboard.

"There!" she said, as if just being in a boat pleased her to no end.

Phew! I said to myself.

Rocking her wheels and turning a little, she maneuvered herself off the boards and into the bow, behind the mast. She rested one arm on the rolled-up sail on top of the boom. "This is perfect!" she said. And then, winking: "Don't worry, I'm not sailing off without you. You're the skipper!"

"That would make you the crew," I said, surprised that she'd gotten herself situated so quickly.

"Aye-aye," she said. "And I don't mind saying I'm a pretty darn good crew! I had a lot of practice way back when."

I pulled the boards aside and stepped carefully into the boat myself. From the compartment beneath my seat, I got out two orange life jackets and gave one to Hazel, which she snapped on, while I put on mine. Since I'd begun sailing, I'd never had anyone crew for me—not Walter, certainly not Lizzy, and not even Dad. My sailing books said the crew's main job is to move with the skipper from one side of the boat to the windward, or upwind, side whenever the boat turns into the wind. That's how you keep your boat balanced. But how in the world would *this* crew do that? What would keep Hazel, like a ball in a box tilting back and forth, from always rolling to the downwind side and eventually tipping us over?

"The brakes on your chair are on, right?" I asked.

She pointed to the two small levers that she'd already pushed to lock her wheels. "And for good measure, could you tie my chair to the mast?" she said. "On the water, you never know what's coming"—which is what I was thinking about, too.

With an extra length of rope, and using a couple of double half hitches, I lashed the metal supports on the back of her chair to the mast, so she was still facing the stern. "Ready? You still want to do this?"

She gave me the thumbs up sign.

I checked the wind indicator. A light breeze was coming off the bay. We were on the downwind side of the dock, so I untied the stern line from its cleat and pushed the stern away from the dock to point us into the breeze, with the bowline still attached. Standing right beside Hazel, I pulled down on the halyard and raised the rustling sail as high as it'd go. The boom just cleared her head.

"Thanks," she said, "I was wondering about that. My head. It's the best part I've got left!" She laughed. "So I'd rather not lose it. Not yet."

I cleated the halyard. I pulled in the fenders. I untied the bowline, and we cast off. Back at the tiller, I steered us away from the dock, while Hazel, as if she'd done this a million times, took the sheet and let it out, then held it as the sail filled, catching the gentlest puff of wind. Then magically, almost silently—with just the murmur of rippled water along the hull—we were under way, Hazel and me, sailing out on the bay.

CHAPTER 18

In the Groove

On maps, our island is shaped like… Well, I don't know exactly what it's shaped like. Maybe some insect or underwater creature with lots of tentacles, hooks, fingers, and arms that reach into the sound, forming many little protected coves and, on the north side, the bay. From side to side, the bay is a mile wide, and from the dock to its mouth that opens into the sound, it's nearly two miles.

"Where shall we go?" Hazel asked.

Leaving the dock, we were on what's called a broad reach, following the shoreline, with a breeze coming over the starboard corner of the stern and pushing us on a course toward the west. We passed the swimming beach with red umbrellas and kids playing on the sand. Soon I could see up the village streets that angle down toward the seawall, with crowded shops, the bank, the firehouse, the bakery, hardware store, and a couple of churches with their tall steeples like needles in the sun.

"Why don't we stay on this heading a while?" I said, proud that I could use a fancy word like "heading" and actually know what it meant. This was easy sailing. Just gliding along, heeling slightly to port. The wind was soft and steady, the waves like long, blue ribbons. There were other boats on the water, but none in our way, and straight ahead in the distance stood Half-tide Rock, a big gray rock, exposed when the tide is low, that I could use as a landmark. Sitting in the stern, I barely had to move the tiller, and I could watch the village pass below the boom, almost like in a movie. I figured we'd keep going like this for a little while, then tack closer to the wind before tacking twice more and heading back to the dock, a short, forty-five-minute trip.

Meanwhile, Hazel made slight adjustments to the sheet, letting it out or pulling it in, so the sail stayed tight and rounded. "This course is fine with me," she said. Though she was facing backwards, toward me, she seemed to know exactly where we were and where we were going. She breathed deeply, as if to suck in the warm, salty air and hold it as long as she could. She tilted her face up toward the sun. "Rusty, isn't this lovely? Isn't it great just to be alive?"

A bird landed on the very top of the sail, right next to my wind indicator on the mast.

"Look at the gull!" I said.

"Yes. But that's not just any old gull," Hazel replied. "It's a Laughing Gull. See its orange beak, its black head, and the white circles around its eyes. And wait 'till you hear it call!"

A moment later, the bird made a sound that I'd often heard but hadn't paid much attention to: a group of notes, at first short and sharp, then lengthening out and getting louder, that really did sound like a kid laughing. *Ha-ha-ha-hah... haah... haaah... HAAAAH!*

"*Ha-ha-ha-hah... haah... haaah... HAAAAH!* to you, too!" Hazel called to the bird, as if they were sharing a joke.

Tossing back its head, the gull laughed again and flew off.

"Laughter—remember that," Hazel said, and I couldn't tell if she was talking to herself or to me, or to both of us.

Now the west end of town passed lazily alongside us: the big, three-story houses of the summer people, with wraparound porches, balconies, and thick chimneys. Next came the slow-swaying grasses along Crab Creek. Then the golf course with its little blue flags and green fairways. Then came the Medical Center and hospital. And then the ferry landing with its two rows of tall pilings, the ramp between them, and the long, metal accordion gate that a man opens when the ferry docks to let the cars and passengers get off and other cars and passengers come aboard. Just then, the ferry was out on the sound, heading away toward the mainland, a curl of smoke behind it.

With her free hand, Hazel pulled from her pocket that brass compass that was usually on her shelf at the cottage. She opened the lid and held it on her palm. "We have a northeast wind at sixty degrees. And you're holding a nice, steady course," she said, "even with the tide running in and with a little cross current." It was awesome, the things she knew and noticed. She put the compass away and brushed some strands of hair from her eyes. We sailed without talking until she said, "Aren't we getting close to Half-tide Rock?"

I said yes and that soon I planned to turn upwind, close-hauled for a little while. "Close-hauled" was another of those words that I'd learned from my sailing books.

She said, "Good! I love sailing close to the wind.

Let's do it!"

So I pushed the tiller, turning the rudder, and we veered away from the village and out toward the middle of the bay. Hazel pulled in the sheet, and the wind and waves, which grew stronger, came from the bow and starboard. I had to sit on the side-deck to keep us balanced. I set us on a course toward Taylor's Point, a mile away, where the lighthouse rises above the rocks and the sound begins—though I wouldn't actually go *that* far. We were sailing faster now, the wind in my face, ruffling the sleeves of Hazel's windbreaker, and we sliced neatly through the low waves.

Looking off at the hills, some with farms and green fields, Hazel talked again about sailing with her dad when she was my age: how he'd use that brass compass, peering through the little hole in its flip-up lid to determine their exact direction... and, oh, how she loved to crew for him. "We worked together, like hand in glove," she said. "I could see in his face what he was thinking, so I'd trim the sail a half second before he'd ask me to. Sometimes he could read *my* mind, as well. 'Let's shake a leg,' he'd say, meaning, *Let's go faster*, my favorite thing, so I'd move forward, sit out as far as I could, and then we'd really be hauling! Some nights, we'd anchor in little coves that only he knew about. We'd eat sandwiches, oranges, and Hershey bars that he'd brought aboard. Sometimes he'd get out his old guitar and in his low voice sing 'The Tennessee Waltz' or 'Walking my Baby Back Home,' as the sun went down behind the mainland. When it was dark, the sky was so wide and speckled with light. We'd watch for falling stars, and when we'd see one, he'd say, 'Make a wish,' and my wish was always the same—that those times would last forever." Hazel stopped for a moment, like she could almost hear her dad singing and see those stars. Then she went on: "If the weather was warm and calm, we'd sleep in our clothes right on the boat, and in the mornings I'd feel the dew in my hair."

As she spoke, I, too, could almost hear that singing, see those stars, and feel the cool, morning dew. Who wouldn't want that to last forever? I just listened to her and kept us on course. As the breeze stiffened, the shoreline behind us got smaller and smaller, and the lighthouse grew taller. When we were about half way to the mouth of the bay, as far out as I'd ever sailed, I figured it was time to tack and start heading back.

I looked around to make sure no other boats were near us. I picked out a new landmark about ninety degrees off our course, a clearing in the woods on the east shore. Then I said, "Ready about!" which is what you say to your crew before you turn into the wind and cross it.

But Hazel yelled, "No! Not ready!"

I thought she'd spotted something, a floating board or a boat I hadn't seen, that might have been in our path. "What's wrong?"

"Nothing. But can't we just keep going like this? It's wonderful! Rusty, we're in the groove right now!"

She was right. When you're sailing upwind, there's a narrow lane, not too close to and not too far off the wind, when your boat is sailing perfectly, when the wind is flowing smoothly around both sides of your sail, when you're sitting out, but not too far, when you're moving quickly but under control, and when you're best using what's blowing against you to help pull you forward.

Sailing like this would be easier if the wind wasn't always shifting. But we were doing it. We were a team—me watching the wind indicator, moving the tiller to keep us in the groove, and Hazel, clenching the sheet in both hands, keeping the sail trimmed just right. We bashed through waves that bounced us up and down and sprayed the side of my face and the back of Hazel's head. It was exciting and a little scary. Behind us, we left a bubbling wake, and the shoreline to the west sped by so fast that I hardly noticed how far from the marina we'd come. "Hold onto your hat!" Hazel said, though neither of us was wearing one.

Surprisingly soon, the lighthouse rose before us with the red stripe around its middle and its bright, turning light at the top that you can really see at night. Closer yet was the floating bell buoy, a low pyramid of iron beams with a big bell in the middle. Rocking on the waves, its loud *gong-gong* also warns boats away from the rocky point, where the big waves from the sound exploded. We were so near that we could hear them now.

"Ready about!" I said again. I didn't want to get *too* near.

And this time, Hazel said, "Ready!"

I called, "Hard-a-lee!" and pushed the tiller toward the sail, so the rudder turned us into the wind. All in one motion, I crossed to port, knees bent, ducking beneath the boom, and passed the tiller behind my back from one hand to the other. For a second, the sail luffed, flapping like a flag, until, as we came to the other side of the wind, it swung smoothly to starboard, where Hazel held it, pulled all the way in. We didn't miss a beat. No fumbling around. No nervous under- or over-steering. Instantly, the sail cupped the wind like a hand. Instantly, we heeled to starboard and shot off close-hauled. Right in the groove again!

CHAPTER 19
Planing

We were way out on the bay now, almost into the sound. The wind was steady and even stronger, whipping up Hazel's hair and making me sit out farther. The waves rolled. Some whitecaps came at us. It was more exciting and scary. On this course, we were clipping along, skirting the mouth of the bay, but not making much progress back toward the village, which now was a distant cluster of shapes nestled at the base of Prospect Hill.

Hazel had that eager look in her eyes. "Have you ever tried a beam reach?" she asked, now shouting over the waves. "That's when the wind comes straight from the side. That's when you're *really* sailing!"

No, I said, I hadn't done that—and I wasn't sure that we should.

She said we could try, if I wanted. "It'll put us on a

better heading. And after that, we can run home with the wind!"

Usually, I'm a cautious person. I've tried to sail only in mild weather. At school, I've never raised my hand in class, and I always sit back by the door. I've never tried out for the school musicals or sports, and I sure don't enter the Math and Science Fair.

So it says something about how charged-up I was that I said to Hazel, "Okay, let's do it." A beam reach. And I also liked the sound of the other thing she'd mentioned: that we could "run home with the wind."

"All right then," she said, looking me in the eye. "Here. Now you take the sheet." She held the line out toward me.

"What?" This surprised me.

"Just take it for a moment. Here. Hold it."

"Why?"

"It's important. You should feel this, all of it, when we turn." She put the sheet in my hand. She pointed toward the tiller. "Now go ahead."

Slowly I turned us toward the east and a little south, until the wind, according to the indicator, was coming right at my back, directly to port, and—WHOOMPH!—it hit us, as hard as that gust had hit me some weeks before. For a split second I held onto the sheet, fighting it, but I remembered what Hazel had said after I'd capsized—that sometimes you have to "let the wind have its way"—and I let it go, which went against my every instinct, like I was giving up or giving in. The sheet, whizzing, flew from my hand. The boat pitched. The boom swung wildly to starboard. The sail thrashed like clothes on a line in a thunderstorm. On the port side, the waves hit us broadside, right up to the toe-rail. But I kept the tiller centered, and we didn't capsize—at least not yet.

"That was good!" Hazel yelled. "We're still upright! We're in business!"

She grasped the sheet that was still whipping around and wrapped it partially around the arm of her wheelchair, so she could handle it better. Very carefully, she pulled the sail in about half way... and now we were moving like I'd never moved before. A beam reach! It was crazy!

"Why don't you let out the sheet a little?" I called. "To slow us down!"

She gave me a sharp look. "Is that an order?"

I'm not very good at giving orders. "No, not exactly."

Then she actually *pulled in* the sail a touch more, so we caught *even more* wind and went faster and faster, down through the valleys, then up, up, and over the crests of the waves. Still tied to the mast, Hazel's wheelchair, like everything, tipped to starboard. "Wheeeee! Ya-hoooo!" she yelled like a kid on a roller coaster.

We were going so fast and heeling so much that I had to hike out as far out as I could, practically lying down backwards, with the tops of the waves smacking my butt and just the rubber foot straps over my sneakers holding me in the boat. The mast and boom seemed to groan with the strain. Water splashed all over us and streamed up on the starboard deck. With all her might, Hazel pushed herself toward the port side of her wheelchair, hiking out as far as she could. The whole world seemed tilted now. And leaning way out above and sometimes in the cresting waves, I could feel the sail stretching and actually bending the wind, and the boat wanting to veer off and slow down, but with my hand gripping the tiller with all my might, I could feel the rudder knifing in and, along with the keel beneath the hull, keeping us more or less on course.

"Bravo!!" Hazel yelled.

And just then, I felt *everything*: the wind, the water, the sun and salt, every stretching or clenching muscle, every inch of shivering skin, every gulping breath, every hair soaked to the root!

And by the looks of her, as she gritted her teeth and gripped the sheet, Hazel seemed to be feeling the same, her hair all wild in the wind. "Yahoooo!" she yelled again and again. And I was yelling with her.

Then an even stranger thing happened.

We were going so fast, we were sailing so well, that the boat, accelerating, rose up *on top* of the waves—*planing* it's called, a kind of skiing—and for an instant I swear we were actually flying. We were off the earth! It was like we were in a whole different place, everything left behind. The waves didn't matter. Math didn't matter. Lizzy's orders and mean comments didn't matter. Dad's moments of forgetfulness didn't matter. Even whatever was happening with Mom seemed far away. Just the big *whooshing* sound of the wind.

Then with a thud, we were back on the water, and a moment later Hazel said in a weak voice that I could hardly hear, "That's enough. We should turn for home." Suddenly she looked exhausted. Her cheeks were chalky, her eyes red with the salty spray. Her shoulders slumped. Her hands shook. She was an old lady in a wheelchair, trying to catch her breath.

What is she doing out here? What are we doing out here?

I turned the boat downwind, straight at the village.

"Why don't I take the sheet?" I said, and without a word Hazel handed it to me. While still holding the tiller, I eased the sail all the way out so it ballooned in front of us, and now we were sailing with the wind and waves, at about their speed. We were "running," but except for the village getting bigger and bigger, it was as if we weren't moving at all, the waves just standing all around us.

For that whole ride back, we didn't speak. Near the marina, I turned 180 degrees, directly into the wind, and let the sail luff. Then I put out the fenders, and we drifted toward the dock, where Jack, in his soiled cap and baggy overalls, threw us a line. He must have seen us coming.

"That's some rig you got there," he said, pointing at the rope lashing Hazel's wheelchair to the mast. "Did you have a good sail?"

Hazel and I glanced at each other. What a mess we were! Our hair stuck out all over the place. Our clothes and life jackets were drenched. "The best sail of my life," Hazel said. "This Rusty here is a pro."

CHAPTER 20

Shaking Hands

When I'd tied up the boat, Jack insisted on getting in and pushing Hazel in her wheelchair up the ramp to the dock. Then I rolled up the sail, pulled up the rudder, left our life jackets to dry, and Hazel and I headed back to her cottage. She pushed the rims of her wheels, while I trudged beside or behind her, feeling exhausted in a way that was different than just being tired, as if something had drained out of me—and maybe out of both of us. As we were going up the gentle slope toward the gate on her brick path, she slowed almost to a stop, though I could tell she was still trying hard to push. I opened the gate. And for the first time, without either of us saying a word about it, I put a hand on one of the plastic handles of her chair, and with just a little forward pressure, I helped her through the gate and up the path until it leveled off in her front yard.

We went inside her cottage, where, as always, Marigold greeted us. In the kitchen, our half-eaten sandwiches were still on the table, and my backpack hung from the back of my chair, though it seemed that they'd been there longer than the two and a half hours that we'd been out sailing. Maybe a thin cloud had passed in front of the sun, or maybe it was just that late-August sense of summer fading away, but the things in the cottage looked different somehow, as if they were things that I was remembering as well as seeing right then. Hazel had gotten out of her wheelchair and, hobbling with her cane, followed me into the kitchen, where I picked up my pack and put it over my shoulder. From her purse on the counter, she pulled out some folded bills held together with a paper clip.

But now, as she stood there all wet, wrinkled, and rumpled, I didn't want to take them from her. "I haven't done any work today," I said. "The money's yours. I didn't earn it."

"Yes, you did. You took me sailing. If you didn't, I'd have had to hire someone else to do it."

"But that's what I do for fun."

"Well, for me," she said, "it was more than just fun."

And as for me, I'd have to say the same, though I couldn't say exactly what it was that had been more than fun. What I did know was that it wasn't work. "The money's yours," I said again. "And besides, you've already given me other things. Like the painting, for instance."

"No. I insist." She was standing like a fence post again. "And I also insist that you take next week off, through Labor Day. You'll need to spend that time with your family. And with your mom, especially."

"But…" I hadn't expected this.

"No buts about it," she said. "That's an order. And I'm the skipper *here*. Right?" She slid the bills into the small, rear zipper pocket of my pack and said, "It's after five. You'd better head home…" And then with that old sparkle in her eyes: "Or I'll have to pay you overtime."

Through the stacks of magazines, folders, and albums, and passing those polished bookcases, we moved to the front door and stood there awkwardly.

I wasn't sure what to think or say. Things seemed to be happening quickly—too quickly—sliding away, like I might not be able to hold them again. "Maybe I can come back and keep working some days after school starts," I said.

Hazel looked at me warmly, but didn't say anything. For a while, she just stared as if taking me all in, every bit of me, and making a photo of me in her mind. I had an odd sense that she knew something I didn't.

"You've grown!" she said all of a sudden, like she hadn't noticed before.

"Not much," I said, "according to our tape measure."

She just smiled to herself.

Then she did another thing that I wasn't expecting. She put out her free hand to shake mine. And we shook. It was the first time we'd ever touched, a moment that you might think was creepy.

As I've said, her hands were bony, veiny, wrinkly, and they trembled. But her grip was strong, as strong as mine, and I didn't want to let go any sooner than she did.

"Good luck, Rusty. Take care," she said as she released my hand, and I turned to go out the door.

CHAPTER 21

Homecoming

When I got home that evening, Dad had just arrived with four red roses. "One for each of us," he said, "as we'll all be together again." Then he, Lizzy, and I arranged them in a vase with flowers that Lizzy had picked from Mom's garden, and we put them at Mom's place at the kitchen table. At supper, none of us argued at all, and that night was another when nobody slept and the green glowing hands of the clock on my bureau barely moved as I kept wondering, *What will Mom be like?*

Will she be changed?

Will she look different?

Will she need to stay in her room? And what will it be like for me?

In the morning, we were all in the kitchen as the sun came up, Lizzy getting ready for camp and me for my last day of summer school. Dad, who'd be leaving before us on his long trip to pick up Mom, wore a brand-new blue-striped shirt and his khaki pants with a crisp crease that Lizzy had ironed in. On his neck were a couple of tiny red marks, where he'd nicked himself with his razor.

"Run the dishwasher before you go," he said to Lizzy and me as we finished our cereal. "Remember your chores when you come home. Make sure there's plenty of water in the vase. Russ, remember to comb your hair. And no arguing when she gets here. Please."

He looked at his watch for about the fifth time in the last ten minutes and grabbed his keys off the rack. He hugged Lizzy and me and said, "See you for supper." Then we followed him out to the porch, where we waved as he drove away with his elbow out the window and his shirt sleeve ruffling in the breeze. Not long after that, when we were heading out the door, we heard the long, low blast of the ferry horn.

• • •

Twelve hours later, as the sun hung above the trees on the west shore of the bay, Lizzy and I were standing behind the accordion gate at the ferry landing. We were looking toward the mainland across the water that was a lot calmer than we were. At summer school that day, Mrs. Kaminski had made it official, or pretty close to that. In the hall, she'd pulled me aside and said, "Congratulations, Russell!" She told me that I'd passed the course, that sometime around mid-summer I'd "suddenly caught fire" and had "made great progress," and that now I could start sixth grade with my usual classmates—my final grade would soon arrive in the mail. After school, I stopped in to see Walter, who had just returned from camp. When I told him I'd passed, he yelled, "Yes!" and we high-fived and played some pretty intense ping-pong in his garage. At home, I spent the rest of that afternoon doing my chores, which didn't seem as bad as usual. I emptied the wastebaskets and set four places at the table, and I also weeded Mom's garden, while Lizzy made her special meatloaf with strips of bacon on top. Then, even though we were a half hour early, we ran down to the ferry slip, me in clean shorts and a T-shirt, and Lizzy in jeans and a sleeveless blue blouse she'd just put on. Now we were waiting and waiting, checking and rechecking the time on our watches, peering out across the wide water.

How many times have I seen this? How many times has anyone who's lived on our island seen it?

At first it's just a tiny flat box, like a matchbox, far out on the surface, with a tiny rectangle sticking up on its port side, and that thin curl of smoke above it. As you look, it doesn't seem to change at all, until you turn away for five minutes and then look again. Now it's slightly bigger, and you start to see things that you couldn't see before: the flat box on the bottom is darker; the rectangle on top is white. You turn away again, trying hard not to peek, and when you finally turn back, it looks like a barge, with water frothing up in front, except that no tugboats are pushing or pulling it, and the white rectangle is taller than any cabin you've seen on a barge. You turn away. You turn back again. And now you can actually see it moving, coming right at you, getting bigger and clearer. The white rectangle has windows and a door at the top—it's the pilothouse—with a little ladder leading up to it, and on its roof a flag flutters and antennae sprout up, with gray and white gulls swooping all around. On the starboard side stands a puffing smoke stack, and on the deck, the windshields and humped tops of cars shimmer in the sun. And soon you can really hear and feel it: the deep throb of the engine, and then the rich, salty stink of churning water as the propellers reverse to slow the boat down.

It has always been like this. Every time. Except that *this* time, the whole process seemed to take forever. And now at the open bow of the ferry, behind a mesh fence like a tennis net, Dad and Mom were standing together, waving to us, she in her green blouse and long, flowing skirt, and with her hair, which looked longer now, streaming back in the wind. She was squinting, and in her sandals she stood on tiptoes—just as we were standing on tiptoes, as if that would help us see her better.

Closer and closer the ferry came, churning, puffing, and throbbing, now squeezing between the two tall rows of pilings on either side of the landing. When at last, with a *thunk*, the boat docked, and Dad went to get into the car, and some men had looped the thick ropes around the giant cleats on the pier, and the metal ramp had come down with a terrific *clank*, and another man had pulled aside the fence and the gate… That's when Mom came across, and we ran to meet her with our hands stretched out as far as they'd go, and she took each of us into her arms and held us so tight that I could feel her fingers pressing into my back, like she'd never let me go.

• • •

In the car going home, Mom sat quietly in the front with Dad, who asked us how our day had been, which of course got Lizzy going the way she did when she was excited. She just had to tell Mom how at camp she'd led some long, dangerous hike that only she could lead, how she'd given first aid to some kid who scraped his knee, and how they'd bushwhacked through the woods and made it back safely.

While she went on like this, I kept my eyes on the back of Mom's head. As well as longer, her hair looked a shade lighter. Had she colored it? Had she been in the sun? And there was something else about her, a faint, sweet smell that I couldn't place. Was it new? Or some shampoo or soap that just seemed new because I hadn't smelled it in a while? Halfway home, she turned to glance back at me, as if to make sure I was still there.

Going up our porch stairs, Dad took Mom's hand, and when he opened the door, her other hand went to her chest, and she paused before going in, like she was pleased but also a little uncertain, which I guess is what we were all feeling.

Inside, Mom took a deep breath and said, "Meatloaf!" She took another breath when she walked into the kitchen and saw the vase of flowers. "They're beautiful!" She ran her fingers along the edge of the counter, the table, and the rounded wooden back of her chair, remembering, it seemed, by touching things.

Dad set her luggage bag on the floor. Carefully he put his arm around her waist. "Welcome home," he said.

• • •

At supper, Lizzy kept plowing ahead with her stories, and Mom ate slowly, listening but not saying much, as though she needed to do just one thing at a time while she got used to being home again. Meanwhile, I didn't know if I should put on the kettle for her tea, or if Mom would get up and put it on herself, like she always had. Or maybe she didn't want any tea. Maybe that was something that was different, and maybe that was why she hadn't touched the cup at all. She seemed so calm in a determined sort of way.

When we'd finished supper, Dad said to her, "It's been a long trip. Do you want to rest?"

Mom said no, she was okay, and she helped Lizzy and me load the dishwasher, which at most is a two-person job, so we kept bumping into each other, saying "Whoops" and "Sorry," and putting in the dishes every which way.

Later, while Dad was downstairs, and Lizzy was on her phone with friends, and I was trying to read in bed, I heard Mom's steps on the stairs. She knocked gently on my door, though it was open. "Mind if I come in?" Her voice seemed shy. In her bathrobe and slippers, she looked tired but pretty, her hair combed, wavy, and tucked back behind her ears. She pulled my desk chair up close to my bed and sat down. She smiled in that way that always made me feel safe, her brown eyes looking right at me. I closed my book and placed it on the nightstand.

"I noticed that someone weeded my garden while I was gone," she said. "Could that have been you?"

I nodded.

"I also noticed that my flowers are still growing, which means that someone watered my garden. And someone must have gotten my cup ready for tea, which I'll make tomorrow. Could that have been you, too?"

I nodded.

"Thanks, Rusty. Thanks for everything. And for being so patient."

I had the sense that she had more to say but couldn't. Her bottom lip trembled, and so did mine. I figured I might ask about those horses she'd taken care of at Woodhaven and the one she called Zephyr, but the words wouldn't come for me either.

Finally she said, "So how did summer school end up?"

We were both happy she'd changed the subject. "Pretty good," I said. "I passed. I think I'm going to get a B!"

Her face lit up. "Wonderful! You must be so proud. So am I. Can you tell me about it?"

Something snagged in my mind. How could I explain how I'd gotten better in math? How could I explain a lot of things? How could I explain Hazel and me? I looked away. "I guess I just got the hang of it."

When I glanced back at Mom, she'd also looked away, her face seemed thoughtful, and her eyes had settled on Hazel's painting on the wall behind me. She tilted her head. "Where did you get this? It's extraordinary."

"What?" I asked, though I knew what she was talking about.

"This painting."

"I got it from the lady at the Art Barn."

"Hazel?"

"Yes."

"You bought it?"

"Not really."

"What do you mean?"

I couldn't avoid telling her now. "Well, I worked for her, at her cottage, during the summer."

"You did? You didn't mention that in your letters."

I was quiet.

"Did she *give* this to you?"

I nodded.

"It's remarkable. Such feeling in it! She must really love sailing."

"Yes," I said. But I couldn't say anymore.

I could see that Mom wanted to ask more questions. Instead, she stopped, as though she sensed my awkwardness in talking about my time with Hazel, and I think she felt awkward hearing about it, too. Like her time at Woodhaven, it was something that Mom and I hadn't shared, like a space between us that had never been there before.

"Well, she must think very highly of you," Mom said, getting up. She bent over and kissed me lightly on the top of my head.

I turned off my lamp.

"See you in the morning," she said. "Sleep tight."

CHAPTER 22

Autumn

During that week before Labor Day, Mom took Lizzy and me shopping a few times—pencils, pens, and notebooks for both of us, new jeans for me, and this totally grossed me out: Lizzy got her ears pierced. With a needle!

Then after Labor Day, the summer vanished like it'd never happened. The summer people left. Their big houses went dark and quiet. Except for the guys swinging metal detectors over the sand, the beach was empty, the lifeguards' tall chairs lying on their sides, dragged off behind the storm fences. Just a few cars came and went on the ferry, and most of the sailboats and yachts disappeared from the bay. The place was ours again.

When I began sixth grade, my own days also felt different, as if I'd stepped through some invisible door that closed behind me. Lizzy now went to Conklin High on the other side of the island, so we didn't walk to school together. My afternoons were busier. Walter and me, we actually joined the ping-pong club that met on Tuesday and Thursday afternoons. On other days, we walked to his house, or we'd go out biking, sometimes up the steep path and beyond the cemetery, where we'd leave our bikes and climb to the top of Prospect Hill. Strangely, I did very little sailing as those weeks went by. It's hard to explain. It was like I didn't *have* to do it anymore. Though I finally had the money, I didn't buy that mooring buoy I'd had my eye on. I didn't sit for hours reading my sailing books. After a heavy rain, I didn't immediately go and bail out the hull. For days, I wouldn't set foot in my boat.

Meanwhile, Mom seemed pretty happy. While every Wednesday night she met with what she called her "support group" and every Friday she had a phone call with her counselor at Woodhaven, by the beginning of October you could almost forget that she'd been so sad and had been away for most of the summer. Still, I wouldn't say that everything with Mom was just like it used to be. There was still that space between us, those things we wouldn't talk about, and she seemed to be watching herself and making a point of doing certain things that would keep her feeling all right. She walked on the beach every day after breakfast. She took a part-time job at the Green Thumb Garden Center. It was as if she was saying, to herself and to us, that even though things can really go haywire, they can still turn out okay.

And what about Hazel? Like so much else, she now seemed part of that vanished summer, almost a part of another *me*, some fifth-grade kid I'd left behind on the other side of that invisible door. I didn't see her anymore.

At odd moments, though, I did think about her—like when I'd turn off my lamp and hear gusts of wind rattling my window. How was she doing? How was Marigold doing? With the fall weather, was Hazel making fires in her fireplace? How was she getting wood to her hearth? Who would rake her leaves and clean her gutters?

Once, when Walter and I were sitting up on Prospect Hill, he actually *made* me think about Hazel. Tossing a pebble over the ledge, he said, "I heard you spent a lot of time working last summer for that old lady who sells stuff in that little garage in town. Is it true?"

Surprised, I could feel my face getting warm and red. If I told Walter about Hazel, what would he think? Would he tell anyone else? I didn't know other kids who were friends with an old lady, and it's not like I could say that she was my aunt or my grandmother or something. "Well, it was just a job," I said. "You know, for the money."

Then around the middle of October, we were walking from school on Bayshore Street, taking a slightly different route than we normally took to his house. Passing the crosswalk where I'd turned so many times that summer before, I looked down Oak Lane where the leaves of the chestnuts, oaks, and especially the maples were turning color…

And there she was: Hazel in her wheelchair, rolling away from us, down the lane, through the patches of yellow-orange sunlight, her arms sticking out like chicken wings, and pushing herself along. She had a canvas bag, loaded probably with groceries or library books, hanging over the right handle of her wheelchair. From a distance, she looked pretty much as she always had, her shoulders slumped but her neck held straight and high. Her white head bobbed slightly with every push of her wheels. The only thing different was a handmade sign, the size of a bumper sticker, stuck on the leather back of her chair:

THIS VEHICLE MAKES
FREQUENT STOPS
BACK OFF!

As I read those words, I had to laugh to myself. I could hear her saying them in her gravelly voice and with that gleam in her eye. Then for a moment she hesitated, like she was tired or flustered, and her hands slipped on the rims of her wheels. Her arms went slack. She came to a stop. Pulling herself together again, she continued very slowly on her way.

I stopped and almost called out, *Hazel! It's me, Rusty! Do you need a hand?*

But something stopped me—I didn't know what—and I didn't say anything.

"What's wrong?" Walter asked, turning, a half dozen steps ahead of me now. He hadn't seen Hazel at all.

"Oh, nothing," I said, my mouth going dry. I was moving again and leaving Oak Lane behind us. "So what do you want to do this afternoon?"

CHAPTER 23

Indian Summer

That Halloween was the first when I didn't feel like going out trick or treating, even after Walter and I had planned out our vampire costumes, which involved plastic fangs and lots of catsup.

"Are you feeling okay?" Mom asked me right after supper, when it'd gotten dark outside. "It's always been one of your favorite holidays." She put her hand on my forehead. "You don't seem to have a fever."

"I'm fine," I said, pushing her hand away. "It just seems like a little kid's thing to do, knocking on everybody's door for some lousy piece of candy."

"But you'll miss all the fun."

"It's a waste of time!"

She gave me a doubtful look. "Rusty, what's bothering you? You've been grouchy for a while now."

"Nothing!" I said. I went and lay on the living room couch. I watched a stupid TV show while Lizzy went out to some Halloween dance with her hair like a waterfall of corkscrews, and Dad in his ridiculous skeleton costume answered the doorbell with our salad bowl of Tootsie Rolls in his hands.

That "Nothing!" I'd said to Mom, like the "Oh, nothing" I'd said to Walter a few weeks before, wasn't exactly true. In fact, as time went on and the less I saw of Hazel, the more weird and jumpy I felt, and the more I kept remembering: the feel of her bony, trembling hand; the sound of her cane tapping the floor; the stacks of magazines; the maps on her walls; the taste of fresh, ice-cold lemonade; the way her eyebrows pinched together when she was fascinated by something I'd said; the way her hands had slipped on the rims of her wheels, and the way I'd said "Oh, nothing" and walked away... Now it was hard to stop thinking about her.

She was especially on my mind on the following Saturday, when I biked down to the marina and took my boat out for a last sail before I'd bring it in for the winter. It was one of those warm, Indian summer afternoons that, except for the fallen leaves and the nearly empty bay, felt more like the middle of June than the beginning of November. Wearing only a T-shirt, windbreaker, and jeans, I stepped into my boat for the first time in a couple of weeks. I bailed out a few gallons of rainwater, rigged the tiller, put on my life jacket, raised the sail, and cast off.

There was a steady, mild, offshore breeze, and I decided to head straight toward the lighthouse. Farther and farther out I went, the air fresh, the sun warm, the boat gliding right along, as if it could read my mind. Then, as I approached the bell buoy and the lighthouse, I did something I'd never done before. I jibed to starboard, toward the mouth of the bay. Slowly I sheeted in as I started the turn, then centered the boom and tiller as the stern crossed the wind. I switched hands and moved to the other side. I let the sheet out, braking it evenly, the boom swinging softly to port, as the sail filled and I completed the turn.

I couldn't believe it! I did it so naturally!

Bravo!! Hazel would have said, as I glanced up at my wind indicator, checked my new heading, and trimmed the sail. I could practically see her sitting in her chair behind the mast, the sun skating on the rims of her wheels, her windbreaker rippling, her hair all crazy, and her face turning from the sun to me. She'd be so pleased and excited.

Keep going on this tack as long as you want, she'd say. Don't let anything stop you, Rusty. This is lovely. You never know when you'll get another chance like this.

So I kept going and going, past the bell buoy, past the lighthouse, past the rocky point, right out through the mouth of the bay and into the sound, where the wind was still gentle, the waves low, and everything seemed so big and wide. I saw no other boats, not even the ferry. Behind Nichol's Point, the village disappeared, the church steeples disappeared, and even Prospect Hill was gone. The sky was blue, with streaks of white jet trails. No gulls circled overhead. The mainland, now a gray pencil line, stretched way, way out there. And farther still, to the north and east, just a few degrees off my heading, I saw a sort of opening, a place where the mainland disappeared, and the sky and the water seemed to come together—which must have been the ocean.

I'd gone far enough. I was due home for supper before dark, so I turned and tacked back into the bay. Suddenly, I wanted to tell Hazel all about everywhere I'd gone and everything I'd seen and done. She was the only person I knew who'd really understand.

I tied up at the dock and dropped the sail. The sun was dipping behind the hills. Hazel, I knew, would be home by then. She'd have closed up the Art Barn hours before, and she'd be reading the paper, maybe doing the crossword puzzle in her armchair before getting herself some supper. *What a surprise!* she'd say when she'd open the door, though she might not be completely surprised. *Marigold, look who's here! It's Rusty! What's up kid? Welcome! Have you had supper? Come on in!*

I pedaled across the parking lot and up Bayshore Street. I turned onto Oak Lane, swirling up leaves behind me. I fast-walked my bike up the narrow, overgrown brick path, through the gate, and across the front yard where the grass was knee-high again and there was that sweet, yucky smell of apples rotting on the ground. I leaned my bike against the trunk of the tree and, breathing hard, I knocked on Hazel's front door.

CHAPTER 24

What Has Happened Here?

But as I knocked, nobody called *Come on in!* or came to let me in. I knocked again, harder. I heard Marigold meow from inside, but still nobody came. I stepped back to take a good look at the cottage windows. The flowers in the boxes were shriveled and gray. Though it was dusk, no lights shone in the living room. I searched the ground for a note that might have fallen off the door.

There was nothing.

Now I called Hazel's name, and just Marigold replied, meowing louder, pleading it seemed. I pulled on the gull's beak and opened the mailbox. I yanked out a couple letters and fliers, a magazine, and the day's newspaper. *That's strange,* I thought. Every day Hazel brought in her mail and the paper before lunch.

All at once, I was sweating. I lifted the mailbox

and found the key beneath it, where it always was, on top of the standing log. I put the key in the lock, turned it, and opened the door.

Inside it was cold and dark and, still meowing frantically, Marigold lay herself over my feet so I could hardly move. I put down the letters and newspaper and picked her up. With one arm, I carried her, while with the other, I felt my way through the dim stacks of albums and magazines to Hazel's reading chair. I turned on the standing lamp. A paperback lay tented on the arm, like she'd just put it down. But no one was sitting there, and no one was anywhere else in the room, which didn't seem to have changed since I'd last seen it, two whole months before. There were the bookcases, packed to the gills. There on the other walls were all the postcards, photos, and maps. There was the record player that was still and quiet. There was that familiar mixed-up smell of old rugs, the litter box, and ashes in the fireplace. There on its peg hung Hazel's cane, like a long question mark. And there a step away stood her wheelchair, its sides squeezed together, as if it'd been pushed out of the way and nobody was using it anymore.

What has happened here?

Quickly I checked the kitchen, bathroom, and

bedroom. Nobody there. Nobody in the studio either. Back in the kitchen, I saw something I hadn't noticed before, probably because it was so familiar, because it'd always seemed to be there and *still* was there, waiting for me: my plaid napkin with that shiny, closed-U-shaped shackle, like a belt around its middle.

Then I noticed something else: Hazel's glasses upside down on the floor beneath the table. A broken plate was down there too. And her chair wasn't in its usual place, but spun around and closer to the wall, as if someone had fallen against it.

There's been some emergency. Where is she?

Then I knew. She must be at the Medical Center out on Nichols Point Drive, where Mom always took us for shots and once when Lizzy broke her arm.

What should I do? I could ride home—I was already late—and say nothing about Hazel. Or I could tell Mom and Dad everything and maybe they'd call the Medical Center—or maybe they wouldn't. What mattered most was that I get to Hazel, and if I cut across the golf course on my bike, I could be at the Center in ten minutes. Something told me to hurry, even if this would get me in trouble.

I found my phone and called home. I'd never told

a big lie like this before. I told Mom that I was invited to Walter's house for supper. I told her that yes, I'd remember to use the light on my bike, and she said, "Okay. Thanks for calling. Have a good time. See you later."

As fast as I could, I filled Marigold's bowls, one with dry food, the other with powdered milk and water, which she practically dove into. I grabbed Hazel's glasses. From the studio, I took a handful of colored pencils and one of Hazel's small sketch pads. In the living room, I grabbed her paperback, found the newspaper page with the crossword puzzle, folded it, and stuffed everything into Hazel's canvas grocery bag, which I slid over my shoulder.

"I have to go," I said to Marigold. I turned off the lamp, went outside, locked the door, and slipped the key back under the mailbox.

CHAPTER 25
The Hospital

Over Prospect Hill, the moon rose like a silver dollar, as I sped around the smooth, flat putting greens and along the fairways that unfurled in the narrow beam of my headlight. With the night, everything felt like fall again. The rushing air chilled my hands and face. At times, bare tree branches crisscrossed the sky, and dry leaves crackled under my tires. Finally, way out on the edge of the golf course, I reached the secret path that Walter and I had discovered, the one through the gap in the chain-link fence alongside Nichols Point Drive.

A few minutes later, after leaving my bike beside a pine tree, I was outside the small roofed area where cars let people off to go into the Medical Center lobby through a wide, glass double door that opens automatically. On either side of the lobby are two wings: to the left the clinic, to the right our tiny hospital, each a single story high and each with about ten identical windows lined up in a row, like a ladder turned on its side. For a minute, I stood still and tried to catch my breath. I'd never been in there alone. Would they let me in? I didn't see any kids in the lobby. Just some nurses in loose blue uniforms going back and forth, and a receptionist behind a tall counter.

Without a mirror or comb, I straightened my hair as best I could. Then I walked through the double door.

Inside was a thick smell, like boiled broccoli, and in an open room around a corner I could see and hear a huge TV, as five or six people in pajamas and robes watched or slept, slumped in sofas or wheelchairs. I was sure none of them could be Hazel.

"Can I help you?" It was the receptionist. Her black hair was shaped like a helmet. Her makeup made her face look pale, and her eyes were as sharp as a teacher's on cafeteria duty. Like most year-round people on the island, we must have seen each other somewhere—walking on the street or in the checkout line at the Stop & Shop—but I couldn't place her.

"Yes. I'd like to see Hazel," I said, trying to sound like I belonged there.

"Hazel who?'

I realized that in all the time I'd known her, I didn't know Hazel's last name. She'd never mentioned it, and if I'd seen it on the front of letters or anywhere else, I hadn't remembered it. "I'm not sure," I said to the receptionist. "But I think she's here."

"Well, what's *your* name?"

"Rusty."

"No, I mean your last name. Maybe it's the same as hers. You must be her grandson, right?"

"No."

"Great-grandson?"

"No."

"Then how do you know her?"

"We're… friends," I said, trying to figure out the best way to describe us.

The receptionist raised an eyebrow, like she didn't believe me.

"Maybe you could tell her I'd like to visit. I brought some pencils and her sketch pad. And her glasses, too." I held the bag open for the receptionist to see. "Could you tell her it's Rusty? She'll know who I am."

"She's very sick, you know. This is a hospital."

"Then she *is* here, right?" Why hadn't she told me in the first place?

The receptionist made a tired face. "Yes, we have a Hazel. Hazel Perkins."

"Can I see her, please? That sign says Visiting Hours, and I'm a visitor. There's forty-five minutes left."

"That sign's for family members," she said, emphasizing the last two words.

"Well, what if Hazel doesn't have much family? What if they're on the other side of the country?"

"You're awfully determined," the receptionist said. "Let me ask her nurse. You sure you want to see her?"

"Yes."

On her phone, she called a number and spoke briefly in a low voice. What I heard was, "Yes… Says he's a friend… Has her glasses… Maybe a neighbor's kid… I've seen him around." Then she seemed to answer some questions: "No, nobody's visited her that I know of… I had a call from a son and daughter. They'll be on the ten-o'clock ferry in the morning… No, nobody else… You sure?… All right."

After she'd finished, the receptionist said to me, "Sign in here." She handed me a pad of lined paper. I wrote 7 p.m. and signed by the X, the first time I'd signed something official, like Mom or Dad signing a check. She pointed to my right. "Down that hall.

Beyond the curtain. The last room on the left. As I said, she's very sick."

Along the yellow-painted, cinder-block hall stood a couple of big, steel machines on wheels with lots of wires, buttons, and dials that gave me the shivers. There was a silver trolley with dozens of shelves holding trays where that smell of broccoli came from. A doctor in a white coat, his shoes squeaking, passed me in the opposite direction. In the rooms on either side, I saw people in chairs or sitting on beds that propped up their backs, with their food on a special table that reached over their laps. In other rooms, I saw people my parents' age helping older people eat. In other rooms, as I kept on walking, I saw people lying down, sleeping or just looking at the ceiling, with silver bed rails on both sides of them, like they weren't allowed to get out.

I came near the end of the hall. A heavy curtain hung across it in green folds which I pushed aside and went around. Behind it, what was left of the hall seemed darker and emptier. No machines. No trolleys. No TVs. A special, quiet place. I'd expected to find a nurse here, but there were only three doors, one on the right, the other on the left, and a fire exit straight ahead.

The door on the left was open a few inches, and for a second, shaking, I stopped in front of it. Would it be better to find Hazel here, or not to find her anywhere at all? Would she even want to see me? Or might she even be too sick to want anything anymore?

I pushed open the door which didn't make a sound. Inside was Hazel. It was definitely her. But she wasn't like I'd ever known her.

CHAPTER 26

Sailing Away

She was lying on a bed with her head slightly tilted up and a tan blanket pulled up to her chin, as if she might have been cold. Her eyes were closed. Her face, without any particular expression, was almost as white as her hair. From the wall, a clear plastic tube circled her head right above her ears and went into each of her nostrils. Another tube ran down from a sack of liquid on a pole and disappeared beneath the edge of her blanket where some wires snaked off in a different direction. She looked tiny. She was silent. And here's the thing that really got me: She didn't move at all—except if you watched with all your might, you could see the blanket slowly rising and falling, like waves on the bay when you can't feel a breath of wind.

This room, I think, was different than the others. A soft light glowed directly above the bed. The air smelled like the inside of a Band-Aid box and not like broccoli. Behind Hazel's head, the wall had lots of sockets and a couple of monitors that beeped very faintly and blinked with colored numbers and moving lines that looked like hills and valleys. On the opposite side of the bed from me, a chest of drawers stood as high as the side rail, and on top was a plastic pitcher and a paper cup with a bent straw in it. Beside the chest of drawers was an empty chair, so I went around the end of the bed and sat down. I put the paperback, crossword, pencils, pad, and Hazel's glasses on top of the chest, and I just watched her. I didn't know what else to do. I didn't know what I *should* do. Everything was just so weird. From the chair, I could see that the liquid from the sack went into Hazel's arm though a needle beneath some clear tape. Where it went in, her skin was the color of eggplants, but she wasn't bleeding. The veins on her arm were blue and forked like roads on a map. Her hand was turned up and open, her fingers curled the way you'd hold a baseball—the same hand that had gripped the sheet when we'd gone sailing, the same one that had painted her paintings, the same that I'd shaken when she'd said, "Good luck, Rusty. Take care."

A nurse came in with one of those fancy new thermometers. She said hi in a warm, gentle voice.

"You must be Hazel's friend. You're her first visitor. Thanks for coming. She may not be able to talk, and she might not seem to know you're here, but I have a hunch she'll understand whatever you say, and she'll appreciate that you've come." Then to Hazel, she said, "Time for your temperature again."

Without her eyelids moving, Hazel opened her mouth slightly and said in a slow, weak voice, "Thirst-y." It was as if her mouth wasn't quite working.

"You're talking!" the nurse said. "Good. That's progress. Hold on, honey." She put one hand in Hazel's hand and with the other slid the round end of the thermometer across Hazel's forehead. Then she made a note on a clipboard, which she returned to the holder on the end of the bed. "Did you know that you have a visitor?" she said to Hazel. "A secret admirer. A handsome young man. Maybe he can give you a drink of water."

It seemed to take a moment for this to sink in. "Mal-colm?" Hazel said, her voice still very slow. Her eyes cracked open and she looked around, as though she didn't know where she was. Malcolm, I remembered, had been her husband, the man in the straw hat.

"No, it's me," I said. For some reason, I was whispering. "It's Rusty."

She turned to look in my direction. "Charlie?" Charlie was her son.

"No. Rusty." This was very strange. "Can I get you some water?"

She nodded yes, her eyes still bewildered.

I poured water and put the cup into Hazel's hand. Trembling, she managed to get the straw to her lips and drink.

"Thanks," the nurse said to me, smiling. "You have a nice touch. You're really helping her, even if she doesn't recognize you." She patted Hazel's arm and said to me, "Have a good visit. I'll be down the hall. If you need me, press that button beside her pillow. I'm never far away." Then she left the room, pulling the door almost shut behind her.

"More?" I asked Hazel.

She shook her head no, and I took the cup and put it back on the chest of drawers.

After a long moment, she said, "Marigold," as if she'd been thinking about that word a while and had hauled it out of a deep well. Maybe she might be waking up a little, I thought, clearing the cobwebs in her head.

"Marigold's at home," I said. "She's fine. She has plenty of food and milk for today. She's probably sleeping in your reading chair."

With her hand, Hazel was touching her ears, eyes, nose, and cheeks, like she was trying to make sure they were hers. "What… happened?"

"I don't know."

"Where… am… I?"

"We're at the hospital."

She didn't seem to understand.

"Something must have happened to you at home," I said, "and you're here at the hospital to get better."

She kept looking at me. "Malcolm?"

"Rusty," I said again. "Remember, you and me?"

She didn't say anything.

"Remember? We ate watermelon. We had a seed-spitting contest. I chopped down the high grass in your yard. You made lemonade with real lemons. We went sailing together."

Her forehead got more wrinkly. "Dad?" She still didn't understand.

Then I got an idea. I picked up Hazel's glasses, opened them, and slid them onto the bridge of her nose, with the curved ends over the plastic tubes that went around her ears. I took the pad and a pencil and, leaning over the side rail, I drew a stick figure of a boat: a long trapezoid for the hull, with a straight vertical line for the mast, and a big right triangle for the sail. "My boat," I said, holding the pad right in front of her. But she didn't understand.

Now above the boat I drew the sun, a circle with beams shooting out, and in back of the sail I drew long, swooping parallel lines. "Wind," I said, and blew my breath across the picture. But she still didn't get it.

So I drew myself in the stern of the boat, a circle on a crossed neck and shoulders, and then I drew Hazel, another circle on crossed lines, behind the mast in an h-shaped chair with big wheels. I even drew the spokes of the wheels and her hair in messy curlicues. "Me and you," I said, tapping each of our figures on the pad with the pencil. "Rusty and Hazel. In my boat. Sailing. Remember?"

This made her eyes get wider, and she moved her neck like she wanted to lift her head, but she couldn't. Instead, she slowly brought her hand up toward the pencil, her whole arm trembling again and shaking the tube that went from her arm to the sack on the pole. So I put the pencil into her fingers, which closed around it, as if it was the most natural thing, that way you're supposed to hold a pencil.

"Do you want to draw?" I asked.

She nodded, and I held the pad right there.

Then, aiming it, she put the pencil point in front of the boat, and still shaking like crazy and pushing the point forward to the side of the pad, she made big, up and down squiggly lines. "Waves," she said.

"Yes!!" I said. "Waves. Big waves! And sun. And wind. Me and you, sailing!"

"Sail-ing…" It was like a word she was feeling and trying to remember in her mouth, a shape as much as a sound. And then in the same way, she said, "Rust-y."

"Yes!! That's me!!"

"Sailor," she said after a moment.

"Yes!!… Well, sort of."

And next, I swear the corners of her mouth turned up very slightly, "Pow-dered milk," she said. Then slowly pronouncing each syllable, she got the whole thing out: "Math-e-ma-ti-cian."

I couldn't help laughing aloud, even in that hospital room, with all the tubes, wires, blinking machines, that smell like Band-Aids, and with Hazel just lying there like that.

Her eyelids were getting heavy again. Her hand dropped back to her side, and the pencil rolled from her fingers. "Tell me," she said.

"Tell you what?"

"Tell me… That day."

Now it was me who didn't get it. What was she talking about? What did she want? It made me frantic to figure out. "Tell you what? What day?"

She took in a breath and again said, "That day," her voice getting weaker.

I still didn't get it. I leaned in closer. "What day? Which day?"

And now her whole face squinched up, like she was trying as hard as she could to make me understand before she drifted off. "That day," she said. "Sailing. Tell…"

Then I knew. "That day we sailed together, right?!"

"Yes," she said, smiling and closing her eyes.

So I told her everything. How it'd been a beautiful afternoon with a mild offshore breeze. How I'd arranged those boards and she'd wheeled herself straight into the boat, and how I'd lashed her chair to the mast. I told her how, in that breeze, we'd sailed toward Half-tide Rock, and how the waves were like long, blue ribbons. I told her how, when we'd turned upwind and went farther into the bay, the wind had blown harder, and as she trimmed the sail and I sat out, we'd sailed close-hauled, right in the groove. It was perfect! We were perfect! We'd come about, and soon the whitecaps rushed at us and, skirting along the mouth of the bay, we'd veered and sailed that crazy beam reach—"Remember?"—the waves smacking us, the wind howling, and both of us yelling our heads off, all scared and all alive… And then came that moment of lifting off, a lightness, flying, a sudden smoothness, nothing to bother us, nothing holding us down… And then we'd run home with the wind…

I looked at Hazel. She hadn't changed. Her eyes still shut. Still smiling. Listening. And it seemed that I should just keep going and going, keep talking and telling, keep making everything last and last. So I told her how, just today, I'd jibed under control, without slamming the boom. I told her how I'd sailed farther than I'd ever sailed before, beyond the rocky point, beyond the lighthouse, out of the bay and into the sound, far, far out where I couldn't even see the village, but I could see the place where the sound meets the ocean, where everything was so big and blue and wide… I told her how I could turn now in any direction, at any time, with or against the wind. "I can sail anywhere!"

Though I couldn't hear it, I saw a word forming

on Hazel's lips… and the word, I'm sure, was *Bravo!*

And then like smaller and smaller waves washing in and spreading on the beach, the blanket over Hazel rose and settled, rose and settled, until the nurse came in and gently said, "It's time," and I had to leave.

CHAPTER 27

Marigold

That night I couldn't sleep. The hands of my clock moved so slowly. I kept seeing that blanket rising, falling, rising, falling...

Then early the next morning, Sunday, before Lizzy got up and after Dad had come back from the Stop & Shop with blueberry muffins, he said to me in a low voice as he closed the kitchen door behind him, "I'm afraid I've heard some sad news."

At the stove where she was cooking sausage, Mom put down the spatula.

"It's about Hazel," Dad went on. "You know, the lady you worked for. Evidently, she had a stroke at home yesterday morning. She died last night at the hospital. I'm sorry, Russ."

"Oh, my goodness!" Mom said, turning off the stove. For a second, she looked at me, and she must have seen something in my face that made her come right up and put her arms around me. Then Dad was there, still in his coat, with his arms around both of us. I don't remember feeling anything very particular then, just an overall dullness, like when you have a very bad cold and everything seems so heavy, thick, and far away, and maybe not even happening at all. From somewhere, I heard church bells, and I think I heard waves on the beach.

After a while, I said, "I lied." I'm not sure why I said it then.

"What?" Mom said.

"Last night, I didn't have supper at Walter's. I was with Hazel."

For a second, Mom and Dad didn't seem to breathe, and then they held me even tighter.

"You could have told us," Dad said.

"Yes," Mom said. Then she said something that I hope was true: "You were a good friend to her."

For a while longer, we stayed like that, and I guess I was starting to feel some things, because with a jolt it occurred to me: "Marigold!"

"What?" Mom said again, wiping her eyes with the heel of her hand.

"Marigold. Hazel's cat. She's all by herself at the cottage!"

Mom and Dad looked at each other, and a message seemed to pass between them.

"Shall we get her and bring her here," Dad said, "until somebody comes to take care of her?"

I nodded. He got my sweatshirt from the closet and gave it to me. "Let's go," he said.

Ten minutes later, we found Marigold in a ball in Hazel's armchair, and when she saw me, she came awake in a second and leaped into my arms, digging her claws through my sweatshirt and into my skin, a kind of pain that hurt so bad that it actually felt good. I put my face in her fur, which seemed like the softest thing in the world, and she purred and purred.

On a notepad on Hazel's kitchen table, Dad wrote his phone number and a message: "We're taking care of the cat. Please call." Then he got the litter box from the mudroom and the dry food from the kitchen counter. "Anything else?" he asked me.

I looked around at the pictures on the refrigerator, at the table with the lamp, the container for pills, and my napkin in its special ring. *Everything else* is what I was feeling, and Dad seemed to understand. I put Marigold down for a second, slid the shackle off the napkin, and put it in my pocket. With Marigold zipped inside the front of my sweatshirt and with my arms hooped around her again, we turned and went through the living room, past the shelves, between the stacks of magazines, past Hazel's cane on the peg, and past her wheelchair that was still scrunched up like an accordion. Then we went out the front door.

When we walked into our kitchen at home, the sausage was cooked, and Mom had scrambled eggs. Lizzy, up and dressed for the day, was kneeling on the floor, her eyes sad—for me, I realized. And she was pouring milk into a bowl—for Marigold.

"Oh, she's wonderful!" Mom said, when she saw Marigold's head poking out of my sweatshirt. "Can I hold her too?" She pulled her chair from the table, sat, and smoothed a dishcloth across her lap, making a kind of bed.

I went to her, unzipped my sweatshirt part-way, and leaned over so Marigold might come out. "Go on," I said, "it's okay."

"Yes," Mom said to Marigold. "Yes, come on out. It's okay."

A paw at a time, Marigold stepped onto Mom's lap. She turned around once, twice, testing it the way that bakers knead dough, and finally she lay there, curling herself up, and rubbed her face on Mom's hand.

CHAPTER 28
Zephyr

On the next day, I took down the mast and boom of my boat, disconnected the rudder and all the rigging, and with Mom, Dad, Walter, and Lizzy, lifted the hull out of the shallow water, hauled it to our shed, and set it gently down on sawhorses again. A few days after that, there was a funeral for Hazel, and she was buried in the cemetery on Prospect Hill, where if you go up there you can feel the wind on your face and hear the deep faraway gong of the bell buoy, and at night see the thread of lights along the mainland and the long beam from the lighthouse sweeping in a silvery circle.

Marigold quickly became our family cat—Hazel's daughter said we should keep her. The Art Barn became Zeke's Antiques. At an auction there in mid-November, Mom bought one of Hazel's paintings, and with money from the sock in my bureau, I bought another. Mom's painting is of a calm sunrise on the bay. Mine shows a kid in swimming trunks, wading out into deeper water—and this makes me think of Hazel's cackling laugh: the kid is carrying a blue umbrella. We hung the paintings on either side of the one already above my bed, Mom drilling the holes in the wall, and me hammering in the nails.

Then on a Sunday a week or so later, while Mom was grocery shopping and Dad and Lizzy were upstairs, there was a light knock on our front door. It was Hazel's son, Charlie, who I'd only seen when he arrived at the funeral a little late. He wore a heavy, wrinkled overcoat, and he looked uncertain and shy. He was older than in that photo on Hazel's refrigerator, but I recognized his narrow shoulders, and there was something in his face that reminded me of Hazel's, though I couldn't say exactly what it was.

"Are you Rusty?" he asked.

I said yes, and he said, "My sister and I've been sorting out the things in our mother's cottage. A few had instructions attached, and last night we found this."

He held out a small, square cardboard box, about three inches across and an inch deep. On it, in handwriting that I knew was Hazel's, it said:

For Rusty. He lives in the gray bungalow on 3rd Street.

I took the box and opened it. Inside was the brass compass with the flip-up lid that had belonged to Hazel's dad and that I'd often fooled around with when Hazel and I took our "coffee breaks." Right then, the compass felt heavier than I remembered, but round and smooth as a skipping stone, it still fit right into my palm.

I opened the lid. Around the dial were the familiar points of the compass, like the points of a star—N, E, S, W—and between them the little degree marks. Under the glass, the red needle, as always, swayed when I moved my hand, but kept returning to where it wanted to be, pointing north toward the bay.

Then I saw, taped on the inside of the lid, a tiny typed note that made me squint, then catch my breath and smile:

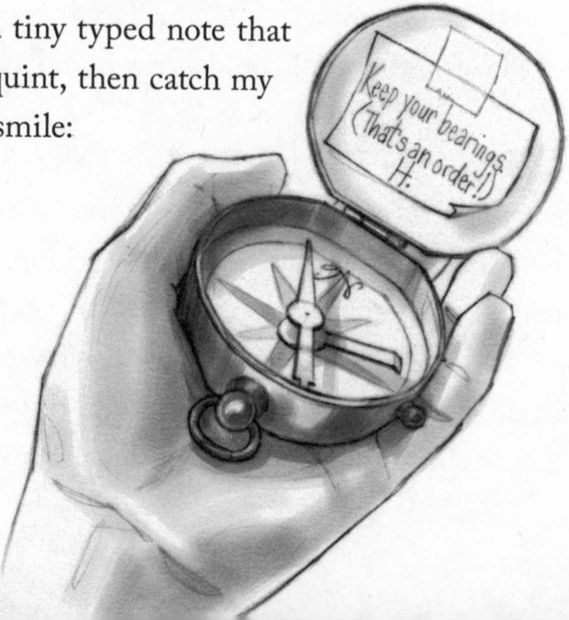

I looked up at Charlie, who was watching me with his weary but curious eyes that seemed to be recognizing something in me. Both of us were missing Hazel.

"Thanks," I said.

He paused. "Thank *you*. You must have meant a lot to her."

I wish that I'd said that she'd also meant a lot to me, but at the moment, I couldn't put it all into words. Instead, I just nodded, and we stood there, not knowing what to do with ourselves.

"Well, I should be getting back to the cottage," he said, taking a step from the door, "to finish packing things up."

• • •

And what happened to Hazel's cottage? A sign soon appeared at the end of the brick path on Oak Lane that said "FOR SALE," which Hazel might have spelled FORESAIL, an eight letter word, she'd be happy to tell you, that means a sail nearest the bow of a boat.

And speaking of words, I decided to name my sailboat Zephyr, a peaceful breeze, after Mom's favorite horse while she was getting better at Woodhaven. It's a good name for a sailboat, and in early December I stenciled it in big letters across the transom.

Then, I got down to some other jobs on the boat. In the afternoons, after I told Mom about my school day and did a half hour of homework, I'd go out to the shed, with the shackle in one pocket of my jeans and the compass in the other. As Marigold squatted on her paws and watched from the doorway, I'd grab some tools and get started. Soon Walter would arrive along with Donny, a new kid in school who's nuts about boats, and we'd talk and work together. We scrubbed the hull with bristle brushes, water, and baking soda. We scraped it with putty knives to get off the summer's barnacles and algae. Next we replaced missing screws in the planks, and with epoxy I filled in cracks. Then we sanded it all smooth and sealed it with varnish, so that this summer my boat will be ready, whenever I'm ready, to go out sailing again.

Zephyr

Glossary of Nautical* Terms

Beam reach Sailing with the wind coming from the side.

Bow The most forward part of a boat (the opposite end or rear of the boat is the **stern**).

Bow handle A metal handle on the bow of a boat.

Broad reach Sailing with the wind coming over the rear corner of the boat.

Buoy An anchored float that warns boats away from hazards or serves as a mooring.

Catboat A boat, like Rusty's, with a single mast close to the bow, and only one sail.

Centerboard A board that can be lowered through the bottom of a sailboat to reduce sideways movement. Instead of a centerboard, Rusty's boat has a keel.

Chock A metal fixture, usually on a boat's deck, with an opening that a rope can pass through.

Cleat A metal fixture, often on a dock, with two horns around which a rope can be wound and tied.

Close-hauled Sailing as close as possible to the wind coming from forward.

Fender A bumper to keep boats from banging into docks or each other.

Grommet A metal ring, in the corner of a sail, though which a rope can pass.

Halyard A rope that raises a sail.

Heel The lean of a boat to one side or the other. It has nothing to do with your shoe.

Jibing Turning the stern of a boat through the wind so that the wind changes from one side of the boat to the other. This is very tricky.

Knot A measure of speed. A knot is one nautical mile per hour, a little faster than one mile per hour.

Leeward The direction opposite to the way the wind is blowing.

Line Any rope used on a boat.

Luffing The flapping of a sail that is no longer filled with wind.

Marina A place where boats are docked.

Mooring An anchored buoy to which a boat is attached by a rope. To **moor** a boat is to attach it to a buoy or post.

***Nautical** Having anything to do with sailors, boats, and sailing.

Nautical mile A measure of distance on water. A nautical mile is exactly 1,852 meters or approximately 6,076 feet. That's 796 feet longer than the sort of mile you're used to on land.

Port The left-hand side of a boat when you're facing forward.

Rigging All the lines and masts on a boat. To **rig** anything is to properly connect all its parts so it works.

Running Sailing with the wind directly behind you.

Shackle A U-shaped metal device for attaching ropes to sails.

Shoal Very shallow water. If you're in a boat, stay away from it!

Slip A place for a boat to moor, often between two docks.

Sound A wide body of water that separates an island or islands from the coastline.

Starboard The right side of a boat when facing forward.

Tacking Turning the bow of a boat through the wind so that the wind changes from one side of the boat to the other.

Trim To adjust a sail.

Wing-and-wing With sails extended on both sides of a boat. Your boat looks a bird with spread wings.

About the Author

photo by B. Tyroler

William Loizeaux's childhood friendship with a feisty aunt who loved painting and sailing inspired him to write *Into the Wind*. He is an award-winning author of books for young readers and adults, as well as a writer of stories and essays. His children's novel *Wings* received the 2006 ASPCA Henry Bergh Award and was the 2006 Golden Kite Honor Book for Fiction.

His memoir *Anna: A Daughter's Life* was a *New York Times* Notable Book, and his novel *The Tumble Inn* was the grand prize winner at the 2015 New York Book Festival. Loizeaux has been writer-in-residence at Johns Hopkins and Boston University. He lives with his wife in Boston, Massachusetts. You can learn more about him and his books at www.williamloizeaux.com

Also by William Loizeaux

For Young Readers:

Wings

Clarence Cochran, A Human Boy

For Adult Readers:

Anna, A Daughter's Life

The Shooting of Rabbit Wells

The Tumble Inn